George Chapman, Ben Jonson, and John Marston's Eastward Ho! A Retelling

David Bruce

Published by David Bruce, 2022.

This is a work of fiction. Similarities to real people, places, or events are entirely coincidental.

GEORGE CHAPMAN, BEN JONSON, AND JOHN MARSTON'S EASTWARD HO! A RETELLING

First edition. August 15, 2022.

ISBN: 979-8201780074

Written by David Bruce.

Table of Contents

Cover Photo for George Chapman, Ben Jonson, and John Marston's *Eastward Ho!* A Retelling

***

https://pixabay.com/photos/model-gift-of-jewelry-goldsmith-2773375/

Educate Yourself
Read Like A Wolf Eats
Be Excellent to Each Other
Books Then, Books Now, Books Forever

***

In this retelling, as in all my retellings, I have tried to make the work of literature accessible to modern readers who may lack the knowledge about mythology, religion, and history that the literary work's contemporary audience had.

Do you know a language other than English? If you do, I give you permission to translate this book, copyright your translation, publish or self-publish it, and keep all the royalties for yourself. (Do give me credit, of course, for the original retelling.)

I would like to see my retellings of classic literature used in schools, so I give permission to the country of Finland (and all other countries) to buy one copy of this eBook and give copies to all students forever. I also give permission to the state of Texas (and all other states) to buy one copy of this eBook and give copies to all students forever. I also give permission to all teachers to buy one copy of this eBook and give copies to all students forever.

Teachers need not actually teach my retellings. Teachers are welcome to give students copies of my eBooks as background material. For example, if they are teaching Homer's *Iliad* and *Odyssey*, teachers are welcome to give students copies of my *Virgil's* Aeneid: *A Retelling in Prose* and tell students, "Here's another ancient epic you may want to read in your spare time."

CAST OF CHARACTERS

TOUCHSTONE: a goldsmith of Cheapside. Touchstones — dark quartz — were used to test the quality and purity of gold and silver alloys. His catchphrase is "Work upon that now!" It means, "You had better think about that!"

MISTRESS TOUCHSTONE: his wife, a gentlewoman.

GERTRUDE: his elder daughter. Touchstone says that she has a "proud ambition and nice — lascivious — wantonness." She wants to become a lady. She can do that by marrying a knight.

MILDRED: his younger daughter. The name includes the word "mild." The name also includes the word "red," which people in this society sometimes used for the color of gold. Touchstone says that she has a "modest humility and comely soberness."

FRANCIS "FRANK" QUICKSILVER: Touchstone's prodigal apprentice. Quicksilver is mercury. In this society, quicksilver was used to treat venereal disease. The Roman god Mercury was the god of thieves. Touchstone says that this apprentice has a "boundless prodigality."

GOLDING: Touchstone's dutiful apprentice. Touchstone says that this apprentice has a "most hopeful industry." Golding is as good as gold.

SINDEFY: Quicksilver's lover, later employed as Gertrude's gentlewoman-attendant. Her name is ambiguous: 1) one who defies sin, or 2) one who defiantly sins.

SIR PETRONEL FLASH: a "thirty-pound knight," engaged to Gertrude. In this society, a "petronel" is a large pistol, aka carbine. He is a newly made knight, and he has purchased his knighthood at a low cost.

CAPTAIN SEAGULL: a ship's captain employed by Sir Petronel to sail to Virginia. "Virginia" was the word then used for the North American coast north of Florida.

SPENDALL, SCAPETHRIFT: adventurers with Captain Seagull. The names suggest "spendthrift."

DRAWER: of the Blue Anchor Tavern in Billingsgate. A drawer is a bartender.

SECURITY: an elderly usurer; bawd to Quicksilver. "Security" is property used to get a loan.

WINIFRED: Security's young wife.

BRAMBLE: a lawyer. "Bramble" is a thorny shrub. Lawyers can get people into or out of thorny entanglements.

SCRIVENER: a writer of contracts.

POLDAVY: a tailor. "Poldavy" is canvas that can be used to make sails.

BETTRICE: a lady's maid.

MISTRESS FOND, MISTRESS GAZER: city women. The word "fond" can mean "foolish." "Gazer" can mean "snoop."

COACHMAN: to Gertrude.

HAMLET: a footman to Gertrude.

POTKIN: a tankard bearer.

FIRST GENTLEMAN, SECOND GENTLEMAN: at the Isle of Dogs.

WOLF: the keeper, aka jailer, of the Counter, a prison for debtors.

HOLDFAST: a prison guard.

FIRST PRISONER.

SECOND PRISONER: His name is Toby.

FRIEND: of the first and second prisoners.

SLITGUT: a butcher's apprentice.

PAGE.

MESSENGER.

CONSTABLE.

OFFICERS.

THE SCENE: LONDON AND VICINITY

NOTES:

Customers wanting to be ferried on the Thames River called "eastward ho!" or "westward ho!" to indicate the direction they wanted to travel.

In the play, eastward is towards Cuckold's Haven, and westward is towards the gallows at Tyburn and Virginia in North America.

East of Goldsmiths' Row was the Wood Street Counter.

Also eastward were Sir Petronel's "land" and "castle."

The play contains allusions to William Shakespeare's *Hamlet*. The names "Gertrude" and "Hamlet" are from Shakespeare's play. This book identifies only some of those references.

This society believed that the mixture of four humors in the body determined one's temperament. One humor could be predominant. The four humors are blood, yellow bile, black bile, and phlegm. If blood is predominant, then the person is sanguine (active, optimistic). If yellow bile is predominant, then the person is choleric (angry, bad-tempered). If black bile is predominant, then the person is melancholic (sad). If phlegm is predominant, then the person is phlegmatic (calm, apathetic, indolent).

Humors are dominant personality characteristics. For example, a person could be optimistic, or angry, or melancholic, or calm, or something else.

A humor can also be a fancy or a whim.

The word "humor" was an in-vogue word in Ben Jonson's day.

In Ben Jonson's society, a person of higher rank would use "thou," "thee," "thine," and "thy" when referring to a person of lower rank. (These terms were also used affectionately and between equals.) A person of lower rank would use "you" and "your" when referring to a person of higher rank.

"Sirrah" was a title used to address someone of a social rank inferior to the speaker. Friends, however, could use it to refer to each other.

The word "wench" in Ben Jonson's time was not necessarily negative. It was often used affectionately.

A "gossip" is a friend or companion or neighbor.

The word "cousin" can mean 1) relative (not necessarily what we call a cousin today), or 2) friend.

A page is a boy-servant.

"Ay me!" is an expression of regret: Alas! Woe is me! Oh! Ah!

PROLOGUE

"Not out of envy, for there's no effect

   "Where there's no cause [nothing to envy]; nor out of imitation,

   "For we have ever [always] more been imitated;

   "Nor out of our contention to do better

   "Than that which is opposed to ours in title,

   [*Westward Ho!* — a play by Thomas Decker and John Webster — was performed in 1604.]

   "For that was good, and better cannot be.

   "And [as] for the title, if it seems affected

   "We might as well have called it, 'God you good even'

   [May God give you a good evening],

   "Only that eastward westwards still exceeds —

   "Honor the sun's fair rising, not his setting.

   "Nor is our title utterly enforced,

   [That is, the action of this play does not always move toward the east.]

   "As by the points we touch at you shall see.

   "Bear with our willing pains, if dull or witty;

   "We only dedicate it to the city."

***

Notes on Prologue:

   The line about being always imitated is a reference to other "city comedies." These are citizen comedies: comedies about the citizens of London.

   The line about titling this play *God You Good Even* is a reference to plays that have commonplace sayings as titles: *As You Like It*, *All's Well That Ends Well*, etc.

   The young general Pompey achieved notable victories in Africa, but the aging dictator Sulla did not allow him to have a triumph in Rome. Pompey said in response, "Honor the sun's fair rising, not his setting."

CHAPTER 1

— 1.1 —

Master Touchstone and Francis "Frank" Quicksilver entered the scene from different directions and met each other.

Quicksilver was carrying pumps (dancing shoes), a short sword, a dagger, and a tennis racket under his cloak. These were items that a gallant — a fashionable young gentleman — would wear or carry.

Golding entered the scene and paced back and forth before a goldsmith's shop.

Touchstone was a goldsmith, and Frank Quicksilver and Golding were his apprentices.

Touchstone asked Quicksilver, "And where are you going now? What loose action are you bound for? Come, what comrades are you to meet with? Where's the supper? Where's the rendezvous?"

"Indeed, and in very good sober truth, sir —" Quicksilver began.

Touchstone interrupted:

"'Indeed, and in very good sober truth, sir'!"

These were words that a Puritan might use.

Touchstone continued:

"Behind my back thou will swear faster than a French footboy and talk more bawdily than a common midwife, and now 'indeed, and in very good sober truth, sir'!"

French footboys — pages — were known for their excessive swearing.

Touchstone continued:

"But if a privy search should be made, with what furniture — what equipment and clothing — are you rigged now? Sirrah, I tell thee that I am thy master, William Touchstone, goldsmith, and thou are my apprentice, Francis Quicksilver, and I will see to where you are running. Work upon that now!"

"Why, sir, I hope a man may use his recreation consistent with his master's profit," Quicksilver said.

Touchstone said:

"Apprentices' recreations are seldom in keeping with their masters' profit. Work upon that now — you had better think about that!

"You shall give up your cloak, though — you are no alderman."

Aldermen were allowed to wear red cloaks. Craftsmen and apprentices wore flat caps. Apprentices wore a cap and gown. Touchstone was dressing like a man of higher social class than his own.

Touchstone removed Quicksilver's cloak, revealing the items that Quicksilver was carrying underneath.

Touchstone then said:

"Heyday, Ruffians' Hall! Sword, pumps, here's a racket indeed."

Ruffians' Hall was a field where much fighting occurred.

"Racket" can, of course, mean "noise" as well as a tennis racket.

Quicksilver said:

"Work upon that now!"

"Thou shameless varlet, do thou jest at thy lawful master contrary to thy indentures?" Touchstone said.

"Indentures" are "articles of apprenticeship."

Quicksilver replied:

"Why, by God's blood, sir, my mother's a gentlewoman and my father a Justice of Peace and of Quorum."

A Justice of Peace heard complaints, and a Justice of Quorum was necessary to have a sitting court and to make determinations about guilt or innocence.

Quicksilver continued:

"And though I am a younger brother and an apprentice, yet I hope I am my father's son; and by God's eyelid, it is for your worship and for your commodity — your profit — that I keep company.

"I am entertained among gallants, true. They call me cousin Frank, right. I lend them moneys, good. They spend it, well. But when they are spent, must not they strive to get more? Must not their land fly? Must not they have to sell their land for cash money? And to whom? Shall not Your Worship have the refusal — the right of first option to buy or not buy?

"Well, I am a good member of the city, if I were well considered. How would merchants thrive, if gentlemen would not be unthrifts? How could gentlemen be unthrifts if their humors — their whims and fancies — were not fed? How should their humors be fed but by white meat and cunning secondings?"

"White meat" is food made from milk, such as cheese.

"White" can mean "having a weak or cowardly character," and "meat" can mean 1) a prostitute or 2) a penis, or 3) a light-skinned person.

According to the *Oxford English Dictionary*, "meat for a person's master" means "someone or something intended for a person's betters, esp. as a source of sexual gratification; someone or something too good to be wasted on a person."

"White" is the lightest color possible, and "light" can mean promiscuous, and so "light meat" may mean the most promiscuous sex partners.

Many gallants visited brothels and contracted syphilis.

"Cunning secondings" are 1) well-prepared second courses, or 2) flattering comments made by yes-men.

Quicksilver continued:

"Well, the city might consider us.

"Suppose that I am going to an ordinary now: The gallants begin to gamble; I carry light gold with me."

An ordinary is an eating place.

"Light gold" is debased coinage. Gold coins had a circle inscribed on them. If the edges of the coin were clipped so much that the circle was broken, the coin was no longer legal tender.

"Light gold" is also counterfeit money.

Quicksilver continued:

"The gallants call, 'Cousin Frank, some gold for silver!' I change, gain by it; the gallants lose the gold and then call, 'Cousin Frank, lend me some silver.'

"Why —"

Quicksilver had been lending money to gallants.

Touchstone interrupted:

" — why? I cannot tell.

"Seven score pounds are thou out in the cash, but look to it, I will not be gallanted out of my moneys."

Quicksilver had been lending Touchstone's money to the gallants, and the gallants had not been paying Quicksilver back.

Touchstone continued:

"And as for my rising by other men's fall, God shield and protect me!

"Did I gain my wealth by ordinaries — eating houses? No.

"By exchanging of gold? No. [That is: By lending money at interest, aka usury? No.] By keeping the company of gallants? No. I hired a little shop, fought low, took small gains, kept no debt book [that is, Touchstone gave no credit], garnished and decorated my shop, for want of plate, with good wholesome thrifty sentences, such as these:

"'Touchstone, keep thy shop and thy shop will keep thee.'

"'Light gains make heavy purses.'

"'It is good to be merry and wise.'"

To "fight low" is a wrestling term, meaning to attack the legs to overthrow opponents and avoid being overthrown oneself.

Touchstone continued:

"And when I was wived, having something to stick to, I had the horn of suretyship ever before my eyes."

Hmm. The word "thing" can mean "pudendum." The word "stick" has another meaning. So does the word "horn."

Also, however, the "something" could be a dowry.

Touchstone continued:

"You all know the device — the illustration — of the horn, where the young fellow slips in at the butt end and comes squeezed out at the buccal."

The buccal is the narrow end: the mouthpiece of the horn.

Hmm. "Slips in at the butt end." Say no more.

The device illustrated the danger of signing or co-signing documents: the danger of guaranteeing that another person's debt would be paid (by you, if need be), or the danger of not paying one's own debt.

Because Touchstone was married, he wanted to support his wife financially, and so he worked at his trade of goldsmithing and he avoided co-signing documents that could make him pay others' debts.

Touchstone continued:

"And I grew up, and, I praise Providence, I bear my brows now as high — I am as important — as the best of my neighbors. But thou — well, look to the accounts; your father's bond lies for you; seven score pounds are yet in the rear — in arrears."

Yeah, unpaid debts can be a pain in the butt.

Quicksilver's father had given his word to pay for Quicksilver's apprenticeship. The bond — written contract — was deposited where it would be kept safe.

Quicksilver said:

"Why, by God's eyelid, sir, I have as good and as proper gallants' words for it [their debt] as any are in London, gentlemen of good phrase, perfect language, surpassingly well-behaved, gallants who wear socks — that is, light shoes or slippers — and clean linen and call me 'kind cousin Frank' and 'good cousin Frank,' for they know my father.

"And by God's eyelid, shall not I trust them? Not trust?"

A page entered. He was looking for Touchstone's shop.

A page is a boy-servant.

"What do you lack, sir?" Golding said. "What is it you'll buy, sir?"

Golding, the good apprentice, was on the lookout for possible customers.

Watching Golding, Touchstone said:

"Aye, by the Virgin Mary, sir, there's a youth of another piece. There's thy fellow apprentice, as good a gentleman born as thou are, nay, and better meaned — from a family that is financially better off.

"But does he pump it or racket it? Does he wear expensive pumps or play tennis? Well, if he thrive not, if he outlast not a hundred such crackling bavins — showy lightweights — as thou are, then may God and men neglect industry."

"Bavins" are "bundles of kindling."

In 3.2, we read that "rash bavin wits, [are] soon kindled and soon burnt."

The page had asked Golding about the location of Touchstone's shop.

Golding now replied, "Here is his shop, and here my master walks."

"Do you have business with me, boy?" Touchstone asked the page.

"My master, Sir Petronel Flash, recommends his love to you and he will quickly visit you," the page said.

Touchstone said:

"He comes here to make up the match with my eldest daughter, my wife's dilling — her darling — whom she longs to call madam. He shall find me unwillingly ready, boy."

Touchstone was ready to meet Sir Petronel Flash, but he did not approve of a marriage between him and one of his daughters.

The page exited.

Touchstone continued:

"There's another affliction, too. Just as I have two apprentices, the one of a boundless prodigality, the other of a most hopeful industry, so I have only two daughters, the eldest of a proud ambition and nice — lascivious — wantonness, the other of a modest humility and comely soberness. The one must be ladified, indeed, and she must be attired just to the court cut and long tail."

The "court cut" is the "court fashion."

"Cut and long tail" also refers to the tails of dogs and horses: docked and undocked.

The words can also refer to dresses with short or long trains.

"... she must be attired just to the court cut and long tail" may mean that Gertrude thinks that she must be attired like a court lady wearing a gown with a long train.

"Cut" also means "vulva," and "long tail" means what you think it means.

If "cut" refers to circumcision, then "cut and long tail" may mean that Gertrude will be attracted to *any* man at court and she will dress accordingly to get one or more of them.

Touchstone continued:

"So far is she ill-natured and antipathetic to the place and means of my preferment and fortune — my occupation as a tradesman — that she throws all the contempt and spite that hatred itself can cast upon it.

"Well, a piece of land she has, it was her grandmother's gift: Let her, and her Sir Petronel, flash out that. But as for my substance, she who scorns me as I am a citizen and tradesman shall never pamper her pride with my industry, shall never use me as men do foxes: Keep themselves warm in the skin and throw the body that bare it to the dunghill."

Readers will find out later that the land was worth two thousand pounds and produced one hundred pounds of income each year.

"I must go and entertain this Sir Petronel."

Touchstone then said to his good apprentice:

"Golding, my utmost care's for thee, and my only trust is in thee. Look to the shop."

Touchstone then said to his bad apprentice:

"As for you, Master Quicksilver, think of husks, for thy course is running directly to the prodigal son's hogs' trough. Husks, sirrah! Work upon that now."

The prodigal son received his inheritance early, spent it, and was so impoverished that he envied hogs their swill. See Luke 15:11–32.

Touchstone exited.

Quicksilver said:

"By the Virgin Mary, faugh — yuck! — goodman flat cap!"

Merchants wore flat caps.

Quicksilver continued:

"By God's foot, although I am an apprentice I can give arms — show a coat of arms, aka armorial bearings — and my father's a justice of the peace by descent, and by God's blood —"

"Bah, how you swear!" Golding complained.

Quicksilver said:

"By God's foot, man, I am a gentleman, and I may swear by my pedigree, God's my life. Sirrah Golding, will thou be ruled by a fool? Turn good fellow [a thief, or a jolly fellow], turn swaggering gallant, and 'let the welkin roar, and Erebus also.'"

Quicksilver saw a lot of plays and sometimes quoted or misquoted them.

Another literary character who does this is Pistol in Shakespeare's *2 Henry IV*, who says, "damn them with King Cerberus, / And let the welkin roar" (Act 2, Scene 4).

Cerberus is the three-headed guard dog of the Land of the Dead.

Quicksilver continued:

"Look not westward to the fall of Don Phoebus [the sun], but to the east — eastward ho!

"'Where radiant beams of lusty Sol appear, and bright Eoüs [Eös, goddess of the dawn] makes the welkin — the sky — clear.'

"We are both gentlemen, and therefore should be no coxcombs. Let's be no longer fools to this flat cap Touchstone.

"Eastward, bully [good fellow]! This satin-belly and canvas-backed Touchstone — by God's life, man, his father was a maltman — a seller of brewers' malt — and his mother sold gingerbread in Christ Church."

Merchants wore clothing that had velvet in the front and inexpensive canvas in the back. They also wore flat caps.

"What do you want me to do?" Golding asked.

Quicksilver said:

"Why, do nothing; be like a gentleman, be idle. The curse of man is labor. Wipe thy bum with testons — sixpences — and make ducks and drakes with shillings."

"Make ducks and drakes with shillings" means to throw shillings and skip them over the water like flat stones: It metaphorically means to waste money.

Quicksilver continued:

"What, eastward ho! Will thou cry, 'What is it you lack?,' stand with a bare pate — head — and a dropping — dripping — nose under a wooden penthouse, and yet thou are a gentleman?"

A penthouse is a projecting roof that provides some protection from rain for people in front of a shop.

Golding could still occasionally get wet, or have a cold, and drops of water would fall from his nose.

Quicksilver continued:

"Will thou bear tankards of water to thy master's house and may thou bear arms? Be ruled by my advice, turn gallant, eastward ho!"

He sang:

"*Ta lirra, lirra, ro.*"

The *Oxford English Dictionary* defines "talio" as "A requiting of like for like, retaliation."

It also defines "talion law" as "the principle of exacting compensation, 'eye for eye, tooth for tooth'; also, the infliction of the same penalty on the accuser who failed to prove his case as would have fallen upon the accused if found guilty."

Chances are, both Touchstone and Quicksilver believed in talion law: Each believed that the other will get what's coming to him, and each believed that he himself would be rewarded.

The Latin *rarus, -a, -um* means "rare, uncommon."

In Elizabethan English, "rare" can also mean "splendid."

Prodigals can end up like the Prodigal Son, envying hogs their swill, but their stories can still, but perhaps rarely, have happy endings: The Prodigal Son's father welcomes him when the son returns. This is a rejection of talion law. This parable celebrates splendid forgiveness.

Quicksilver declaimed:

"'Who calls Jeronimo? Speak, here I am.'"

The quotation is from Thomas Kyd's *Spanish Tragedy* (2.5.4).

Quicksilver then said:

"God's so, how like a sheep thou look!"

"God's so" can mean 1) By God's soul, or 2) catso, aka Italian slang for "penis."

Quicksilver concluded:

"On my conscience, some cowherd begot thee. Thou Golding of Golding Hall, huh, boy?"

He was mocking Golding and calling him a yokel rather than a gallant.

Golding replied, "Go, you are a prodigal coxcomb — a prodigal fool. Am I a cowherd's son because I will not turn into a drunken whore-hunting rakehell — rascal — like thyself?"

"Rakehell?" Quicksilver said. "Rakehell?"

Quicksilver attempted to draw his sword, but Golding tripped up his heels and held him.

"Pish! Bah!" Golding said. "In soft terms — the softest words I can use to describe you — you are a cowardly bragging boy. I'll have you whipped."

"Whipped?" Quicksilver said. "That's good, in faith. Untruss me?"

"Untruss" means 1) release, or 2) undo the fastenings that keep one's breeches up (once his breeches were down, he could be whipped).

Golding said:

"No, thou will undo thyself."

"Undo" can mean "ruin."

Golding continued:

"Alas, I behold thee with pity, not with anger. Thou common shot-clog, gull of all companies."

A "slot-clog" is a fool who is tolerated because he picks up and pays the bill for all.

Golding continued:

"I think I see thee already walking in Moorfields without a cloak, with half a hat, without a band [collar], a doublet [jacket] with three buttons [at least one button is missing], without a girdle, a hose with one point [points were laces that geld up the hose] and no garter, with a cudgel — because you cannot afford a sword — under thine arm, borrowing and begging threepence."

Quicksilver said:

"Nay, by God's life, take this and take all.

"If you take my sword, you may as well take everything I have.

"As I am a gentleman born, I'll be drunk, grow valiant, and beat thee."

He exited.

Alone, Golding said:

"Go, thou most madly vain, whom nothing can recover — can cure — but that which reclaims atheists and makes great persons sometimes religious: calamity.

"As for my place and life, thus I have read:

"'*Whatever some vainer youth may term disgrace,*

"*The gain of honest pains is never base.*

"*From trades, from arts, from valor honor springs;*

"*These three are founts of gentry, yea, of kings.*'"

He closed the shop and exited.

Gertrude, Mildred, Bettrice, and Poldavy the tailor talked together inside Touchstone's house. Gertrude was Touchstone's elder daughter, and Mildred was his younger daughter. Bettrice was a lady's maid.

Poldavy was holding a pretty gown, a Scotch farthingale [hooped petticoat], and a French fall [flat collar] in his arms. These were items of clothing.

Gertrude was wearing a French head attire [a French hood] and a citizen's gown. Mildred was sewing; and Bettrice was leading a monkey after her.

In this scene, Gertrude will change her middle-class city attire for courtly dress.

Like Quicksilver, she curses a lot. Quicksilver often quotes short passages from plays, and Gertrude often sings short snatches of bawdy songs.

Gertrude said:

"For the passion of patience, look and see if Sir Petronel approaches, that sweet, that fine, that delicate, that — for love's sake tell me if he comes.

"Oh, sister Mil, although my father is a low-capped tradesman, yet I must be a lady, and, I praise God, my mother must call me 'Medam.'"

"Medam" is an affected pronunciation of "madam."

"Medam" is also "Me damn."

In other words: "[...] and, I praise God, my mother must call me 'me damned.'"

Or: "[...] and, I praise God, my mother must tell me that I am damned."

Or: "[...] and, I praise God, my mother must call me the one who was damned."

Gertrude continued:

"Is he coming?

"Off with this gown, for shame's sake, off with this gown! Don't let my knight see me in the city fashion by any means.

"Tear it! A pax on it!"

She wanted the gown taken off her quickly, even if it had to be torn off.

The Latin word *pax* means "peace," and it can mean a depiction of the Crucifixion on a gold or a silver tablet that the priest kisses, and it can mean a kiss of peace, but Gertrude was willing to burn her bridges behind her.

"Pax" is an affected pronunciation of "pox."

"A pox on it" is an oath.

Gertrude continued:

"Does he come? Tear it off."

She removed her gown and sang:

"'*Thus whilst she sleeps I sorrow for her sake,*' etc.

The title of the song is "Sleep, Wayward Thoughts," and it is about lustful thoughts.

Mildred, Gertrude's sister, said, "Lord, sister, with what an immodest impatience and disgraceful scorn do you put off your city attire! I am sorry to think you imagine to right yourself in wronging that which has made both you and us."

Gertrude was ashamed that her father made his money as a shopkeeper. It was much more classy to get one's money income from owning land.

Gertrude said:

"I tell you I cannot endure it. I must be a lady.

"You can wear your city attire: coif [hoodlike cap] with a London licket [latchet, aka string that fastens the coif under the chin], your stammel [red wool] petticoat with two guards [ornamental borders], the buffin [a type of fabric] gown with the tuftaffety [taffeta] cape and the velvet lace.

"I must be a lady, and I will be a lady.

"I like some humors [whims] of the city dames well: to eat cherries [a luxury] only at an angel a pound, good; to dye rich scarlet black, pretty; to line a grogram [a type of fabric] gown clean through with velvet, tolerable. Their pure [clean white] linen, their smocks of three pounds a smock [chemise, undergarment] are to be borne with.

"But your mincing niceries — affected niceties — your taffeta pipkins [small hats], durance [a type of fabric worn by city ladies] petticoats, and silver bodkins [long hair pins] — as God is my life, as I shall be a lady I cannot endure it.

"Has he come yet? Lord, what a long knight it is!"

She sang:

"*And ever she cried, 'Shoot home!'*"

She then said:

"— and yet I knew one longer —"

She then sang:

"*and ever she cried, 'Shoot home!'*

"*Fa, la, ly, re, lo, la.*"

"Fa ly" and "Fa lo ly" are both "folly." "La re" is "lare," aka a bird, possibly a seagull. "Fa-la" is a kind of madrigal (a song for more than one voice). "Fallow" is a piece of plowed but unseeded land.

Sir Petronel was, according to Gertrude, long overdue.

A "long knight" may be a sexually well-endowed knight.

"Shoot home" means what you think it means.

As will become known, Gertrude is not a virgin, and she is not pregnant.

"Well, sister," Mildred said, "those who scorn their nest often fly with a sick wing."

A proverb states, "It is a foul bird that defiles its own nest."

"Bow-bell!" Gertrude said. "Cockney!"

Cockneys were born within hearing of the bell at St Mary-le-bow. They tended to be lower-class.

Mildred said:

"Where titles presume to thrust before fit means to second them, wealth and respect often grow sullen and will not follow."

In other words: People who buy titles should first have the means to live in the manner expected of those who have such titles. If they don't first have those means, they lose wealth, grow poor, and lose respect.

Mildred continued:

"For sure, in this I wish for your sake that I was not speaking the truth.

"'*Where ambition of place goes before fitness of birth, contempt and disgrace follow.*'"

A proverb stated, "Pride goeth before and shame cometh after."

Mildred continued:

"I heard a scholar once say that Ulysses, when he counterfeited himself mad, yoked cats and foxes and dogs together to draw his plow, while he followed and sowed salt."

Ulysses, aka Odysseus, did not want to fight at Troy, so he thought up a trick that he hoped would keep him out of the fighting. He pretended to be insane, and he yoked an ox and an ass to his plow and sowed his fields with salt. A Greek man named Palamedes knew that Ulysses was faking insanity, and he placed Ulysses' infant son, Telemachus, in front of the plow. If Ulysses were insane, he would kill his son. But, of course, he was faking insanity and he turned the plow aside and did not kill his son. Ulysses then had to go to Troy and fight. He fought well, and he thought up the idea of the Trojan Horse: the trick that led to the sack of Troy.

The team that pulls a plow ought to consist of evenly matched animals. An ox is stronger than an ass.

Mildred continued:

"But to be sure, I judge truly mad those who yoke citizens and courtiers, tradesmen and soldiers, a goldsmith's daughter and a knight. Well, sister, pray to God that my father does not sow salt, too."

Mildred believed that people ought to marry within their social class.

Gertrude said:

"Alas, poor Mil! When I am a lady, I'll pray for thee yet, in faith, and I'll vouchsafe to call thee sister Mil still, for although thou are not likely to be a lady as I am, yet to be sure thou are a creature of God's making, and may perhaps be saved as soon as I."

As a prefix, "mil" can be a thousandth, or a thousand. A milliliter is one-thousandth of a liter, but a millennium is a thousand years. A "mil" can be small or big, low or high.

Currently, Gertrude regarded Mil — Mildred — as a lowly person.

She then asked about Sir Petronel:

"Does he come?"

She then sang:

"*And ever and anon she doubled in her song.*"

"Double" means to repeat a note but in a different octave.

Another kind of doubling is coupling.

Gertrude then said:

"Now lady's my comfort, what a profane ape's here! What a profane fool!"

"Now lady's my comfort" means "The Virgin Mary's my comfort."

Gertrude then said:

"Tailor, Poldavy, please fit it! Fit it! Is this a right Scot? Does the farthingale clip close and bear up round?"

The farthingale was an item of clothing that fit tightly around a woman's waist. It extended outward from the waist, and the skirt hung from it. Because the farthingale extended outward from the waist, women could not let their arms and hands freely hang down.

"Bear up round" is something that erect penises do.

Poldavy the tailor said, "Fine and stiffly, in faith. It will keep your thighs so cool and make your waist so small!"

A woman would find it difficult to have sex while wearing a farthingale. This would help keep her waist small.

Poldavy the tailor continued:

"Here was a fault in your body, but I have supplied the defect with the effect of my steel instrument, which, although it has just one eye, can see to rectify the imperfection of the proportion."

A "fault" is 1) a defect, or 2) a vagina.

A "steel instrument" with one eye is 1) a needle, or 2) an erect penis.

He put the farthingale and new gown on her.

Gertrude said:

"Most edifying tailor! I declare, you tailors are most sanctified members and make many crooked things go upright. How must I bear my hands?"

The Puritans used the word "sanctified" for saintly and the word "crooked" for sinful.

Hmm. "Members." "Things go upright." Say no more.

She continued:

"Light? Light?"

Poldavy replied:

"Oh, aye, now you are in the lady fashion you must do all things light.

"Tread light, light. Aye, and fall so; that's the court amble."

The word "light" means 1) gracefully, or 2) wantonly.

A lady with light heels is a promiscuous lady: one whose heels are easily spread and raised into the air. The lady would fall backward into the missionary position.

Gertrude skipped about the stage and asked, "Has the court never a trot?"

"No, but it has a false gallop, lady," Poldavy said.

The courtiers, because of their bad characters and many seductions, are galloping toward eternal damnation.

Gertrude sang, "*And if she will not go to bed —*"

Bettrice looked up and said, "The knight's come, indeed."

Sir Petronel, Master Touchstone, Mistress Touchstone, and Golding entered the scene.

Gertrude said:

"Has my knight come?

"Oh, the lord, my band! My collar!

"Sister, do my cheeks look well? Give me a little box on the ear — a little slap on the cheek — so that I may seem to blush.

"Now, now! So, there, there, there! Here he is.

"Oh, my dearest delight! Lord, lord, and how does my knight?"

She kissed him.

Shocking, that, in this society.

Her father, Touchstone, said, "Bah, act with more modesty!"

"Modesty!" Gertrude said. "Why, I am no citizen now. Modesty! Am I not to be married? You would do best to keep me modest now I am to be a lady."

Her last sentence was sarcastic, but events will reveal its truth.

"Boldness is good fashion, and court-like," Sir Petronel said.

Gertrude said:

"Aye, in a country lady — a lady of the county aristocracy — I hope it is, as I shall be."

Knowing Gertrude, she wanted to be a member of the cunty aristocracy.

Gertrude then asked:

"And how does it happen that you came no sooner, knight?"

Sir Petronel said:

"Indeed, I was so entertained in the progress with one Count Epernoum, a Welsh knight."

A "progress" is a visit of the royal court to places in the countryside.

Sir Petronel continued:

"We had a match at the game of balloon, too, with my Lord Whachum, for four crowns."

Sir Epernaum was not likely to exist, and Sir Petronel was unlikely to have played the game of balloon he mentioned.

Epernaum, however, resembles the words "Keep her now" — 'eep 'er nau — and "Capernaum," and it has the same number of syllables as "Petronel."

Sir Petronel has come to marry Gertrude and therefore be able to keep her now — that is, after the wedding.

Or "'eep 'er nau" could mean "Keep her nah." Touchstone would very much prefer that Gertrude not marry Sir Petronel.

Capernaum is an ancient fishing village that was located on the shore of the Sea of Galilee.

Capernaum was humble, but knights are often proud. Knights can be big balls of wind.

Sir Petronel and Epernoum supposedly played a game with a big ball of wind.

The game of balloon was played with a large, inflated leather ball that players hit with their arms, which were protected with a wooden armguard.

Lord Whachum is What-You-Call-Him.

"At baboon?" Gertrude said, mishearing the word "balloon." "Jesu! You and I will play at baboon in the country, knight."

In this society, baboons had a reputation for lechery.

The game of baboon can lead to a baby-boon and a baby-boom.

"Oh, sweet lady, it is a strong play with the arm," Sir Petronel said.

Gertrude said:

"With arm, or leg, or any other member, if it be a court sport."

Hmm. "Any other member." Say no more.

She then asked:

"And when shall we be married, my knight?"

"I come now to consummate it, if your father may call a poor knight his son-in-law," Sir Petronel said.

Touchstone said:

"Sir, you have come."

He did NOT say, "Sir, you are welcome."

In Ben Jonson's society, as well as in our own, the verb "come" can mean "ejaculate."

He continued:

"What is not mine to keep, I must not be sorry to forego. Land worth a hundred pounds in annual rent her grandmother left her; it is yours. She herself (as her mother's gift) is yours.

"But if you expect anything from me, know, my hand and my eyes open together; I do not give blindly.

"Work upon that now."

"Sir, you don't mistrust my means, do you?" Sir Petronel said. "I am a knight."

Knights tended to have means. They needed at least to own a horse, weapons, and armor.

"Sir, sir, what I don't know, you will give me permission to say I am ignorant of," Touchstone said.

Mrs. Touchstone said:

"Yes, you act ignorant that he is a knight!"

She was happy that a knight wanted to marry Gertrude, and she wanted her husband to also be happy about that.

She continued:

"I know where he had money to pay the gentlemen ushers and the heralds their fees.

"Aye, that he is a knight, and so might you have been, too, if you had been anything else than an ass, as well as some of your neighbors.

"If I thought you would not have been knighted, as I am an honest woman I would have dubbed you myself. I praise God I have wherewithal."

King James I often made grants of knighthood in return for money. This was a scandal. Sir Petronel had bought his knighthood.

To "dub" someone is to give that person a new title. Touchstone's wife, if she thought that he would decline to become a knight, could dub him with the title of cuckold. As a woman, she has the wherewithal to do it.

But she could buy for him the title of knight, perhaps, if it is true that she has the wherewithal — the independent income to do it. Later, however, she complains about not being able to get money for Gertrude.

Mrs. Touchstone then said:

"But as for you, daughter —"

"Aye, mother," Gertrude said. "I must be a lady tomorrow, and by your leave, mother — I speak it not without my duty to you, but only in the right of my husband — I must take place of you, mother."

By marrying a knight, Gertrude would rank socially higher than her mother. She would take precedence of her mother: She would do such things as enter a room first. Society people entered rooms in order of social standing.

"That you shall, lady-daughter, and have a coach as well as I, too," Mrs. Touchstone said.

"Yes, mother," Gertrude said. "But by your leave, mother — I speak it not without my duty that I owe to you, but only in my husband's right — my coach horses must take the wall of your coach horses."

To "take the wall" means to "take the best position." A person walking at the side of a street would walk close to the wall to avoid being splashed with mud or dirty water from the street and to avoid the muck in the gutter. When two people going in opposite directions passed each other, the higher-ranking person would take the wall.

Horses tend to be unaware of such societal niceties, but these are court horses.

Touchstone said:

"Come, come, the day — the sun — grows low, it is supper time. Use my house; the wedding solemnity is at my wife's cost. Thank me for nothing but my willing blessing, for — I cannot feign and lie — my hopes are faint.

"And sir, respect my daughter; she has refused for you wealthy and honest — honorable — matches, known good men, well monied, better traded [better established in trade, and with better skills], and best reputed."

Gertrude said:

"Body of truth, chitizens, chitizens!"

She was mocking citizens.

"Chitizens" rhymes with "shitizens."

She continued:

"Sweet knight, as soon as ever we are married, take me to thy mercy out of this miserable chitty; immediately carry me out of the scent of Newcastle coal and the hearing of Bow-bell. I beseech thee, down with me, for God's sake!"

She wanted him to take her down into the country to a better-smelling home and to lay her down in a bed and sleep with her — and to stay awake for a while before sleeping.

Touchstone said:

"Well, daughter, I have read that old wit who sings:

"The greatest rivers flow from little springs.

"Though thou art full, scorn not thy means at first;

"He that's most drunk may soonest be athirst.'

"Work upon that now!"

Everyone except Touchstone, Mildred, and Golding exited.

Touchstone said:

"No, no; yonder stand my hopes."

He was referring to his other daughter, Mildred, and to Golding.

He then said:

"Mildred, come hither, daughter. And how do you approve of your sister's fashion? How do you fancy her choice? What do thou think?"

"I hope, as a sister, that all is and will be well," Mildred said.

"Nay, but, nay, but, how do thou like her behavior and her humor?" Touchstone said. "Speak freely."

"I am loath to speak ill, and yet — I am sorry about this — I cannot speak well," Mildred replied.

Touchstone said:

"Well, very good. As I would wish, a modest answer."

He then said:

"Golding, come hither; hither, Golding."

Golding stepped forward.

Touchstone then said:

"How do thou like the knight, Sir Flash? Doesn't he look big and self-important? How do thou like the elephant? He says he has a castle in the country."

"Pray to heaven that the elephant carry not his castle on his back," Golding said.

In other words, the elephant's wealth may be solely in his clothes. The elephant — a symbol of pretensions to greatness — is the knight: Sir Petronel.

In India, war elephants sometimes carried a fortification on their back.

"Before heaven, very well said!" Touchstone said. "But seriously, how do thou repute him?"

"The best thing I can say about him is, I don't know him," Golding said.

Some people are well worth not knowing.

Touchstone said:

"Ha, Golding! I commend thee, I approve thee, and I will make it appear and make it apparent that my affection is strong to thee.

"My wife has her humor, and I will have mine.

"Do thou see my daughter here? She is not fair, well-favored and pretty, or so — her beauty is only indifferent — which modest measure of beauty shall not make it thy only work to watch her, nor sufficient mischance to suspect her."

In other words: Mildred was not so pretty that men were constantly trying to seduce her, nor was she so ugly that she was forced to constantly look to find a lover.

Touchstone continued:

"Thou are towardly and outgoing, and she is modest and bashful; thou are provident, and she is careful."

"Provident" means "providing for the future," and "careful" means "being frugal now."

Touchstone continued:

"She's now mine. Give me thy hand; she's now thine.

"Work upon that now!"

A man and a woman could join hands and become engaged in a ceremony called hand-fasting.

Holding hands fastened the couple together. Holding hands confirmed the agreement to marry.

"Sir, as your son-in-law I honor you, and as your servant I obey you," Golding said.

Touchstone said:

"Do thou say so?"

He then said:

"Come here, Mildred."

She came.

Her father then said:

"Do you see yonder fellow? He is a gentleman, although he is my apprentice, and he has somewhat to take to — he has some financial resources and some personal qualities worth having.

"He is a youth of good hope and good promise, well friended and related to people with good connections, and he is well parted — he is a man of skill and good qualities. Are you mine? You are his.

"Work you upon that now!"

"Sir, I am all yours," Mildred said. "Your body gave me life, and your care and love gave me happiness of life. Let your virtue still direct it, for to your wisdom I wholly dispose myself."

Touchstone said:

"Do thou say so? Be you two better acquainted."

He then said to Golding:

"Lip her, lip her, knave! Kiss her!"

Golding kissed Mildred.

Touchstone then said:

"So, shut up shop; let's go in. We must make holiday."

Golding and Mildred exited.

Alone, Touchstone said to himself:

"This match shall go on, for I intend to find out and test and prove which thrives the best, the mean and lowly love, or the lofty love. I will find out and test and prove whether fit wedlock vowed between like and like, or prouder hopes, which daringly overstrike their place and means, thrives the best."

A proverb stated, "Like blood, like good, like age make the happiest marriage."

A marriage between Golding and Mildred was a marriage of social equals and a marriage of people with similar good personal qualities and similar ages.

A marriage between Sir Petronel and Gertrude was a marriage based on social climbing.

Touchstone said:

"It is honest time's expense when seeming lightness bears a moral sense."

Gertrude's apparent lightness is likely to give readers a moral lesson. This is a good use of time.

Touchstone concluded:

"Work upon that now!"

CHAPTER 2

— 2.1 —

The time was morning. The previous day, Sir Petronel and Gertrude had been married.

Outside his shop, Touchstone called, "Quicksilver! Master Francis Quicksilver! Master Quicksilver!"

Quicksilver, who was drunk and hiccupping, walked over to him and said, "Here, sir. (Hic!)"

Touchstone said:

"So, sir, nothing but flat Master Quicksilver, without any familiar addition, will fetch you."

"Master Quicksilver" was formal address.

"Francis" in "Master Francis Quicksilver" was a familiar addition.

Touchstone then asked:

"Will you truss my points, sir?"

He wanted Quicksilver to help him tie his hose to his doublet.

A doublet is a jacket.

Quicksilver said, "Aye, indeed. (Hic!)"

Quicksilver tied Touchstone's points, aka laces.

"How are you now, sir?" Touchstone asked. "The drunken hiccup so soon this morning?"

"It is only the coldness of my stomach, indeed," Quicksilver said.

In this society, doctors believed that a cold stomach caused hiccups, one cure for which was drinking wine.

Touchstone said:

"What! Have you the cause natural for it? You're a very learned drunkard. I believe I shall miss some of my silver spoons with your learning."

Quicksilver could steal and then sell Touchstone's silver spoons to get money to spend in taverns.

Touchstone continued:

"The nuptial night will not moisten your throat sufficiently, but the morning likewise must rain her dews into your gluttonous weasand."

A weasand is a throat.

"If it shall please you, sir, we did but drink (hic!) to the coming off of the knightly bridegroom," Quicksilver said.

'To the coming off of him?" Touchstone said.

"Aye, indeed," Quicksilver said. "We drunk to his coming on (hic!) when we went to bed, and now that we are up, we must drink to his coming off. For that's the chief honor of a soldier, sir, and therefore we must drink so much the more to it, indeed. (Hic!)"

In this society, family and friends would escort the bride and groom to their bedroom and often would cause music to be played the next morning to awaken them.

The chief honor of a soldier is to come off victoriously from the battlefield.

The phrases "coming on" and "coming off" have sexual overtones and undertones.

"A very capital reason," Touchstone said. "So that you go to bed late and rise early to commit drunkenness? You fulfill the scripture very sufficient wickedly, indeed."

Isaiah 5:11 states, "*Woe unto them that rise up early in the morning, that they may follow strong drink; that continue until night, till wine inflame them!*" (King James Version).

"The knight's men, indeed, are still on their knees at it (hic!), and because it is for your credit, sir, I would be loath to flinch," Quicksilver said.

The knight's men were kneeling as they proposed toasts.

Quicksilver, to honor Touchstone, would not flinch while drinking a toast but would instead drain the cup.

"I pray, sir, even to them again then," Touchstone said. "You're one of the separated crew, one of my wife's faction, and my young lady's, with whom and with their great match I will have nothing to do."

Touchstone's house was divided into two factions. In one faction were Mrs. Touchstone and Gertrude and Sir Petronel, and in the other faction were Touchstone and Mildred and Golding.

"So, sir," Quicksilver said. "Now I will go keep my (hic!) credit with them, if it shall please you, sir."

"In any case, sir, lay one cup of sack more on your cold stomach, I implore you," Touchstone said.

"Yes, indeed," Quicksilver said.

He exited.

Touchstone said:

"This is for my credit! Servants always maintain drunkenness in their master's house 'for their master's credit.' It is a good idle serving-man's reason."

The wedding of a daughter was an occasion to celebrate, and so servants celebrated it for the master's honor.

Touchstone continued:

"I thank Time the night is past; I never stayed awake to such cost. I think we have stowed more sorts of flesh in our bellies than ever Noah's ark received."

During the Great Flood, Noah and his family survived in their ark, which they had filled with two — male and female — of every kind of animal.

"And as for wine, why, my house turns giddy with it, and there is more noise in it than at a water conduit, aka public fountain."

Servants got water from conduits and carried the water to their employers and their employers' families. Water conduits were a place of much gossip.

Touchstone sighed and said:

"Even beasts condemn our gluttony. Well, it is our city's fault, which, because we commit seldom, we commit the more sinfully. We lose no time in our sensuality, but we make amends for it."

He was using "commit" in the sense of "commit one of the Seven Deadly Sins." Think of Exodus 20:14: "*Thou shalt not commit adultery*" (King James Version).

The Seven Deadly Sins are lust, gluttony, avarice, sloth, wrath, envy, and pride. These sins are deadly because they can "kill" the soul — the divine spirit — that is present in each human being.

Touchstone continued:

"Oh, that we would do the same in virtue negligence and religious negligence!"

In other words: We don't get drunk and overeat often, but when we do, we really get drunk and we really overeat. By "we" is meant "Londoners."

Also in other words: It's a pity that we don't greatly indulge in being virtuous and religious after a period during which we neglect virtue and religion.

Golding and Mildred opened the shop and sat on either side of the stall, which was a table on which were wares for sale.

Touchstone said about them:

"But see, here are all the sober parcels — sober individuals — my house can show.

"I'll eavesdrop and hear what thoughts they utter this morning."

He walked to the side, where he could not be easily seen.

Golding said to Mildred, "But is it possible that you, seeing your sister preferred to the bed of a knight — that is, advanced in social class by being married to a knight — should contain and confine your affections in the arms of an apprentice?"

Mildred replied, "I had rather make up the garment of my affections in some of the same piece than like a fool wear gowns of two colors or mix sackcloth with satin."

Mildred preferred to marry someone of her own social status. She felt that marrying above her social class was like wearing a coat made of a lower-class material such as sackcloth and a higher-class material such as satin. Jesters — Fools — wore clothing made of different colors and of different pieces of cloth.

Leviticus 19:19 states, "*Ye shall keep my statutes. Thou shalt not let thy cattle gender with a diverse kind: thou shalt not sow thy field with mingled seed: neither shall a garment mingled of linen and woollen come upon thee*" (King James Version).

Golding said, "And do the costly garments — the title and fame of a lady, the fashion, and the observation and reverence [deference and respect] proper to such preferment — no more inflame you than such convenience [small comforts] as my poor means and industry can offer to your virtues?"

In other words: Don't you prefer the luxuries of the higher social classes to the small comforts that I can give you?

Mildred answered:

"I have observed that the bridle given to those violent flatteries of fortune is seldom recovered. They bear one headlong in desire from one novelty to another, and where those ranging appetites reign, there is always more passion than reason; no support and no restraint, and so no happiness.

"These hasty advancements are not natural. Nature has given us legs to walk to our objects, not wings to fly to them."

In other words: People who desire rapid social advancement are driven more by strongly felt desires than by reason, which is needed to control desires.

In Plato's *Phaedrus*, 253ff. appears the allegory of the chariot, which represents Humankind's tripartite soul. A charioteer drives a chariot drawn by two horses, which represent passions, aka desires. The white horse represents positive desires, such as the desire to achieve honor. The dark horse represents negative desires, such as the desire for drunkenness. The charioteer represents reason, which is needed to control the desires.

A man may desire to become King, but if his desires are not restrained by reason, he could attempt to become the new King by assassinating the old King. This would be a mistake. Ask Macbeth.

Golding said:

"How dear an object you are to my desires I cannot express, with whose fruition, if my master's absolute consent and yours would grant me, I should be absolutely happy.

"And although it would be a grace so far beyond my merit that I should blush with unworthiness to receive it, yet thus far both my love and my means shall assure your requital: You shall want nothing fit for your birth and education — what increase of wealth and advancement the honest and orderly industry and skill of our trade will afford to any person, I don't doubt will be aspired by me; I will forever make your contentment the end of my endeavors; I will love you above all; and only your grief shall be my misery, and your delight, my felicity."

Touchstone said to himself:

"Work upon that now!

"By my hopes, he woos honestly and orderly; he shall be the anchor of my hopes. Look, see the ill-yoked monster, his fellow."

Quicksilver entered the scene. He was drunk, his laces were untied, he was wearing the flat cap of a tradesman, and he had a towel around his neck.

Touchstone called Quicksilver unyoked because the laces of his clothing were not fastened, and because he was not using reason to control his desires.

Quicksilver said:

"Eastward ho!

"*Holla, ye pampered jades of Asia!*"

He was quoting Christopher Marlowe's *2 Tamburlaine*, 4.3.1.

"Drunk now downright, on my fidelity!" Touchstone said to himself.

Quicksilver said, "(Hic!) Pulldo, pulldo! 'Showse,' quoth the caliver."

"Pull dough" means "knead dough so that it will rise."

Pulling on a soft, doughy penis can also make it rise.

"Showse" is a portmanteau word joining "shoot" and "owse," aka "ooze."

A penis can shoot a kind of ooze.

A caliver is a light gun and shooting a gun can be compared to ejaculation.

There's a reason why a British punk rock band named themselves The Sex Pistols.

"Bah, fellow Quicksilver, what a pickle you are in!" Golding said.

Quicksilver said:

"Pickle? Pickle in thy throat!

"Zounds, pickle? Wa ha ho!"

Quicksilver was drunk because he was celebrating the marriage of Gertrude and Sir Petronel.

"Pickle in thy throat!" may be a reference to fellatio.

"Zounds" means "By God's wounds."

"Wa ha ho!" is the cry of a falconer.

Quicksilver said:

"Good morning, Knight Petronel.

"G'morning, lady goldsmith."

Quicksilver was so drunk that he thought he was talking to Sir Petronel and to Gertrude.

"Come off, knight, with a counterbuff, for the honor of knighthood."

A counterbuff is a counter-blow. When a knight was struck by another person, the knight would lose honor if he did not return the blow.

To a soldier, to "come off" meant to leave the field of battle.

To a lover, to "come off" meant to get off (from on top of) the loved one.

If oral sex by Gertrude can be considered a strike, aka blow, in a battle, the counter-blow would be for Sir Petronel to perform oral sex on her.

Wedding nights can be a comic battle in which the participants compete in giving each other sirrahsexual pleasure.

"Why, how are you now, sir?" Golding asked. "Do you know where you are?"

"Where I am?" Quicksilver said. "Why, by God's blood, you jolthead, where I am?"

A "jolthead" is a blockhead.

Golding said, "Go to! Go to! Come! Come! For shame, go to bed and sleep out this immodesty — this lack of moderation; thou shame both my master and his house."

Quicksilver said:

"Shame? What shame? I thought thou would show thy bringing up. If thou were a gentleman as I am, thou would think it no shame to be drunk. Lend me some money; save my credit."

"Credit" can mean reputation.

Quicksilver continued:

"I must dine with the serving-men and their wives — and their wives, sirrah!"

Quicksilver was the clod-pate: the fool who was tolerated because he picked up the check and paid for all.

"Dine with who you will," Golding said. "I'll not lend thee threepence."

Quicksilver said:

"By God's foot, lend me some money.

"*Hast thou not Hiren here?*"

"Hiren" is a character in George Peele's lost play *The Turkish Mahomet and Hiren the Fair Greek.*

The word also means "hirin," aka "hiring or employment." Yes, Golding had a job, and therefore he must have money that he could lend Quicksilver.

Touchstone came forward and asked, "Why, how now, sirrah? What vein's this, huh? What style of speech is this? What mood is this?"

Quicksilver quoted a line from another play:

"*Who cries on murder? Lady, was it you?*"

This is a line from George Chapman's *The Blind Beggar of Alexandria*, 9.49.

Quicksilver continued:

"How does our master?

"I request thee, cry, 'Eastward ho!'"

"Sirrah, sirrah, you're past your hiccup now," Touchstone said. "I see you're drunk."

"It is for your credit, master," Quicksilver said.

"And I hear you keep a whore in town," Touchstone said.

"It is for your credit, master," Quicksilver said.

This kind of credit was money Quicksilver took from Touchstone to support her.

"And what you are out in cash — what you lack in cash — I know," Touchstone said.

"So do I," Quicksilver said. "My father's a gentleman; work upon that now! Eastward ho!"

Touchstone replied:

"Sir, 'Eastward, ho!' will make you go 'Westward, ho!'"

East of Goldsmiths' Row was the Wood Street Counter.

West of the city of London was Tyburn, famous for its gallows.

Touchstone continued:

"I will no longer dishonest" — he meant 'dishonor' — "my house nor endanger my stock — my property — with your license. There, sir, there's your indenture."

He handed Quicksilver a document.

By giving Quicksilver his contract of indenture, Touchstone was formally firing him.

Touchstone continued:

"All your apparel — that I must know — is on your back, and from this time my door is shut to you. From me be free, but for other freedom and the moneys you have wasted, 'Eastward ho!' shall not serve you."

Touchstone knew about some of Quicksilver's clothing: the clothing that Touchstone was obligated to give his apprentice. But Quicksilver had other clothing, as shown by his pumps in 1.1.

Apprentices who completed their apprenticeships were given certain freedoms that Quicksilver would not now get because he was fired.

Quicksilver said:

"Am I free of my fetters? Rent [Wages], fly with a duck in thy mouth!"

The phrase "to come home with a duck in the mouth" meant "to make a profit."

Quicksilver had lost his employment, and therefore he had lost his rent (wages) and his board (food, such as duck), which Touchstone paid for. His wages and room and board were flying away from him.

Quicksilver continued:

"And now I tell thee, Touchstone —"

Normally, he would call Touchstone "Master Touchstone."

"Good sir," Touchstone began.

Quicksilver recited a line from a play: "*When this eternal substance of my soul —*"

"Well said and well done," Touchstone said. "Change your gold ends for your play ends."

In other words: Instead of working as a goldsmith, go ahead and quote fragments of lines from the plays you love so much.

Also in other words: Exchange bits of gold for bits of plays.

"Gold ends" are fragments of gold.

Quicksilver continued: "*Did live imprisoned in my wanton flesh —*"

"What then, sir?" Touchstone asked.

The next line was this:

"*Each in their function serving other's need,*"

Quicksilver skipped that line and recited:

"*I was a courtier in the Spanish court,*

"*And Don Andrea was my name.*"

The lines Quicksilver had recited were adapted from Thomas Kyd's *The Spanish Tragedy*, 1.1.1–2, 4–5. He had skipped line 3. He did not want to serve the need of Touchstone, and Touchstone did not want to serve the need of Quicksilver.

"Good master Don Andrea, will you march?" Touchstone asked.

"Sweet Touchstone, will you lend me two shillings?" Quicksilver asked.

"Not a penny," Touchstone said.

Quicksilver said:

"Not a penny?

"I have friends, and I have acquaintance. I will piss at thy shop posts and throw rotten eggs at thy sign.

"Work upon that now!"

Staggering, he exited.

Touchstone then said to Golding:

"Now, sirrah, you! Listen, you! You shall serve me no more neither, not an hour longer."

"What do you mean, sir?" Golding asked.

Touchstone said:

"I mean to give thee thy freedom, and with thy freedom my daughter, and with my daughter a father's love. And with all these, I will give thee such a marriage portion — a dowry — as shall make Knight Petronel himself envy thee.

"You're both agreed, are you not?"

Golding would no longer be an apprentice.

Golding was now a journeyman — a skilled worker — in his profession of goldsmithing. In time, he might become a master.

With the dowry, Golding and Mildred could begin their life together.

Golding and Mildred knelt and said, "With all submission, both of thanks and duty."

Touchstone took their hands and helped them rise to their feet, and then he said:

"Well, then, may the great power of heaven bless and confirm you!

"And, Golding, so that my love to thee may not show less than my wife's love to my eldest daughter, thy marriage feast shall equal the knight's and hers."

Golding said:

"Let me beseech you, no, sir. The superfluity and cold meat left at their nuptials will with bounty furnish ours."

In Shakespeare's *Hamlet* 1.2.180-1, appear these words:

"Thrift, thrift, Horatio. The funeral baked meats

"Did coldly furnish forth the marriage tables."

Golding continued:

"The grossest prodigality is superfluous cost of the belly."

Gluttony is one of the Seven Deadly Sins.

Golding continued:

"Nor would I wish any invitement of statesmen and dignitaries or friends; only your reverend presence and witness shall sufficiently grace and confirm us."

Touchstone replied:

"Son to my own bosom, take her and my blessing!"

He then said about Gertrude:

"The nice fondling, my lady sir-reverence, that I must not now presume to call daughter, is so ravished with desire to hansel — to begin using — her new coach and see her knight's eastward castle that the next morning will sweat with her busy setting forth."

A "fondling" is a little fool.

"Sir-reverence" means "saving your reverence." It is an apology for vulgar language (which Gertrude used frequently). "Sir-reverence" also meant "excrement."

Touchstone continued:

"Away she and her mother will go, and while their preparation is making, we ourselves, with some two or three other friends, will consummate the humble match we have in God's name concluded."

Golding and Mildred exited.

Alone, Touchstone said to himself:

"It is to my wish, for I have often read

"*Fit birth, fit age, keeps long a quiet bed.*

"*It is to my wish, for tradesmen, well it is known,*

"*Get with more ease than gentry keeps his own.*"

The gentry — at least the gallants Quicksilver spent time with — tended to be spendthrifts; the tradesmen tended to be frugal. Lack of money problems often leads to better sleep.

He exited.

Alone, Security, an elderly usurer and bawd to Frank Quicksilver, talked to himself outside his house:

"My privy — intimate and familiar — guest, lusty and vigorous Quicksilver, has drunk too deep of the bride-bowl, but with a little sleep he has much recovered and I think is making himself ready to be drunk in a gallanter likeness. He is ready to get drunk like a gallant."

A bride-bowl was a large cup of alcoholic drink passed around to wedding guests.

Security continued:

"My house is, as it were, the cave where the young outlaw hoards the stolen vails — the stolen profits — of his occupation; and here, when he will revel and party in his prodigal similitude and similarity, he retires to his trunks and — I may say softly — his punks."

Punks are prostitutes.

Security continued:

"He dares trust me with the keeping of both, for I am security itself; my name is Security, the famous usurer."

Quicksilver entered the scene, wearing his apprentice's coat and cap and his gallant's breeches and stockings, and pulling on his garters.

Quicksilver's top half was appareled like an apprentice, and his bottom half was appareled like a gallant.

Quicksilver said:

"Come, old Security, thou father of destruction."

The Devil is the father of lies. As a usurer, Security causes destruction for those who cannot pay their debts.

Quicksilver continued:

"The indented sheepskin is burned wherein I was wrapped and confined, and I am now loose to get more children of perdition into thy usurious bonds."

Documents such as contracts of indenture were written on sheepskin.

The sheepskin was a kind of disguise for Quicksilver. As an apprentice, he encouraged gallants to gamble and lose money, thus making them prey for Security. Quicksilver had been a wolf in sheep's clothing.

Although Quicksilver was no longer an apprentice, he still intended to profit from other people's vices.

Quicksilver continued:

"Thou feed my lechery, and I feed thy covetousness; thou are pandar to me for my wench, and I am pandar to thee for thy cozenages and cheats.

"'Ka me, ka thee' runs through court and country."

"Ka me, ka thee" means "Help me, and I'll help you," or "You scratch my back, and I'll scratch your back," or "One good turn deserves another."

Considering the moral characters of these two characters, readers may want to add, "One bad deed deserves another."

Security replied:

"Well said, my subtle Quicksilver. These K's open the doors to all this world's felicity; the dullest forehead — brain — sees it."

The word "keys" was pronounced "kays."

Security continued:

"Let not master courtier think he carries all the knavery on his shoulders. I have known poor Hob in the country, who has worn hobnails on his shoes, have as much villainy in his head as he who wears gold buttons in his cap."

"Hob" was a stereotypical name for a rustic.

"Why, man, it is the London highway to thrift — the quickest way to profit," Quicksilver said. "If virtue would be used, it is used just as a scrap — just as bait — to the net of villainy. They who use virtue simply and sincerely, thrive simply and poorly, I promise. Weight and fashion make goldsmiths cuckolds."

Goldsmiths became cuckolds — men with unfaithful wives — because so much of their time was spent making money: weighing gold and fashioning it into jewelry or other objects.

According to Quicksilver, honest goldsmiths get rich slowly through hard work. If they were to get rich fast through villainy, their wives would be faithful.

Sindefy, Frank Quicksilver's punk and lover, entered the scene, carrying Quicksilver's doublet (jacket), cloak, rapier, and dagger. These were fine items of clothing that were worn by a gallant, not by an apprentice.

"Here, sir, put off the other half of your apprenticeship," Sindefy said. "Take off your apprentice's hat and cloak."

Quicksilver said:

"Well said, sweet Sin! Bring forth my bravery: my finery. Now let my trunks shoot forth their silks concealed. I now am free and now will justify my trunks and punks."

Trunks can be 1) chests for storing such things as clothing, or 2) trunk-hose.

He would now acknowledge his lover and his fine clothing.

These were things that an apprentice was not supposed to have or be able to afford.

Quicksilver continued:

"Avaunt — go! — dull flat cap, then! *Via* — go! — the curtain that shadowed Borgia!"

He threw his apprentice's hat and cloak on the ground.

Cesare Borgia (1475–1507) was known for his ability to disguise himself.

Quicksilver continued:

"There lie, thou husk of my envassaled state.

"I, Samson now, have burst the Philistines' bands and in thy lap, my lovely Delilah, I'll lie and snore out my enfranchised state."

"Bands" are 1) bonds (contracts), or 2) shackles and fetters.

Judges 16 tells the story of Samson and Delilah. She betrayed him by cutting his long hair, which (the hair) was the source of his strength.

Quicksilver dressed himself as a gallant, complete with rapier and dagger.

Gallants followed the then-current style of fighting duels with just a rapier and dagger — no shield.

He then sang:

"*When Samson was a tall [brave] young man*

"*His power and strength increasèd then.*"

Quicksilver then said:

"He sold no more, neither cup, nor can, but did them all despise.

"Old Touchstone, now write to thy friends for one to sell thy base gold ends.

"Quicksilver now no more thee attends, Touchstone."

He then asked Security, "But Dad, have thou seen my running — racing — gelding dressed today?"

Quicksilver was also not supposed to have enough money to own a racing horse.

Security was not Frank Quicksilver's biological father. "Dad" was simply an informal way to address an older man.

The word "dressed" can mean 1) groomed, or 2) prepared for cooking.

"That I have, Frank," Security said. "The ostler of the Cock dressed him for a breakfast."

An ostler, aka hostler, was a person who took care of horses.

The Cock was an inn.

"What, did he eat him?" Quicksilver asked.

"No, but he ate his breakfast for dressing him, and so dressed him for breakfast," Security said.

The ostler had earned his breakfast by dressing, aka grooming, Quicksilver's horse. That is how the ostler made his living.

Quicksilver said:

"Oh, witty age, where age is young in wit,

"And all youth's words have greybeards full of it!"

"But, alas, Frank, how will all this lifestyle be maintained now?" Sindefy asked Quicksilver. "Your position as an apprentice maintained it before."

Quicksilver replied:

"Why, and I maintained my place. I'll go to the court — another manner of place for maintenance, I hope, than the silly city.

"I heard my father say, I heard my mother sing, an old song and a true:

"'*Thou art a she-fool, and know'st*

"'*Not what belongs to our male wisdom.*'

"I shall be a merchant, indeed! Trust my estate in a wooden trough as he does? What are these ships but tennis balls for the winds to play with? Tossed from one wave to another, now under line and low down, now over the house and high up; sometimes hit brick-walled against a rock, so that the guts fly out again; sometimes struck under the wide hazard, and farewell Master Merchant."

In the game of court tennis, which was played indoors, a line on the wall indicated the lower boundary of play. The "house" was a sloping roof that indicated the upper boundary of play. "Bricked-walled" is a corruption of *bricole*, a stroke in which the ball was hit on a side wall and advanced toward the opponent. The hazard was an opening in the wall. Balls hit into them won points.

Tennis balls were made of hair, and when they wore out, they spilled their guts.

Sindefy said:

"Well, Frank, well, the seas, you say, are uncertain.

"But he who sails in your court-seas shall find them ten times fuller of hazard and danger, wherein to see what is to be seen is torment more than a free spirit can endure.

"But when you come to suffer, how many injuries swallow you? What care and devotion must you use to humor an imperious lord? Proportion your looks to his looks, smile to his smiles? Fit your sails to the wind of his breath?"

"Tush, he who cannot do that is no journeyman — no skilled worker — in his craft," Quicksilver said.

Sindefy replied:

"But he's worse than an apprentice who does it, not only humoring the lord, but every trencher-bearer and waiter, every groom and servant, who by indulgence and intelligence crept into his favor and by pandarism into his bedchamber."

Gallants can advance at court by being on friendly terms with lords and with the servants who encourage the vices of their lords and who spy on and gossip about them and who provide them with whores.

Sindefy continued:

"The servant rules the roost, and when my honorable lord says, 'It shall be thus,' my worshipful rascal, the groom of his close-stool, says, 'It shall not be thus,' claps the door after him, and who dares enter?"

A close-stool is a toilet: an enclosed chamber pot.

Some servants gained and exercised power by controlling access to their lords. If you never see a lord, you can't ask him for favors.

Sindefy continued:

"An apprentice, quoth you? It is but to learn to live, and does that disgrace a man?"

Being an apprentice is nothing to be ashamed of: The apprentice is simply learning to make a living.

Sindefy continued:

"He who rises hardly — by facing and overcoming difficulties — stands firmly; but he who rises with ease, alas, falls as easily."

"A pox on you," Quicksilver said, "Who taught you this morality?"

Security said:

"It is owing to this witty age, Master Francis.

"But indeed, Mistress Sindefy, all trades complain of inconvenience, and therefore it is best to have none.

"The merchant, he complains and says, 'Overseas trading is subject to much uncertainty and loss.'

"Let them keep their goods on dry land, with a vengeance — with a curse — and not expose other men's substances to the mercy of the winds, under protection of a wooden wall — the ship's hull — as Master Francis says, and all for greedy desire to enrich themselves with unconscionable gain, two for one, or so.

"In contrast, I, and such other honest men who live by lending money, are content with moderate profit — thirty or forty in the hundred, so we may have it with quietness and out of peril of wind and weather, rather than run those dangerous courses of trading, as they do."

The maximum legal rate of interest that could be charged was ten percent — not thirty or forty percent.

"Aye, Dad, thou may well be called Security, for thou take the safest course," Quicksilver said.

Security said:

"Indeed, I take the safest course — and the quieter, and the more contented, and, no doubt, the more godly.

"For merchants in their courses are never pleased, but instead they are always repining and complaining against heaven. One prays for a westerly wind to carry his ship forth; another for an easterly to bring his ship home; and at every shaking of a leaf, he falls into an agony to think what danger his ship is in on such and such a coast, and so forth.

"The farmer, he is always at odds with the weather. Sometimes the clouds have been too barren; sometimes the heavens forget themselves [and rain at the wrong time, when water is not needed], their harvests answer not their hopes; sometimes the season turns out to be too fruitful, corn will bear no price, and so forth.

"The artificer — the trickster and con-man — he's all for a stirring world; if his trade is too dull and falls short of his expectation, then he falls out of joint."

Quicksilver wanted his trade to be that of a conman.

Security continued:

"Whereas we who trade nothing but money are free from all this. We are pleased with all weathers: Let it rain or hold up, be calm or windy, let the season be whatsoever, let trade go how it will, we take all in good part, even whatever pleases the heavens to send us, provided that the sun does not stand still and the moon keeps her usual returns from new moon and the sun and moon together make days, months, and years."

"And you have good security?" Quicksilver asked.

"Aye, by the Virgin Mary, Frank," Security said. "That's the special point."

Quicksilver said:

"And yet, indeed, we must have trades and tradesmen in order to live, for we cannot stand without legs nor fly without wings, and a number of such scurvy, contemptible phrases and worthless sayings.

"No, I say still and always, he who has wit, let him live by his wit; he who has none, let him be a tradesman."

Security said:

"Witty Master Francis! It would be a pity if any trade should dull that quick brain of yours.

"Do but bring Knight Petronel into my parchment toils — traps of contracts — once, and you shall never need to toil in any trade, on my credit.

"You know his wife's land?"

"Even to a foot, sir, I have been often there," Quicksilver said. "A pretty fine seat and country estate, good land, all entire within itself — that is, it has all that is needed."

"Is it well wooded?" Security asked.

"It has two hundred pounds' worth of wood ready to fell, and a fine sweet house that stands just in the midst of it, like a prick in the middle of a circle," Quicksilver said.

"A prick in the midst of a circle" is 1) an arrow or pin in the center of a target, or 2) a penis in a vagina, and, possibly, 3) an erect clitoris (if the vulva is regarded as a circle).

Hmm. Sir Petronel's wife's "land" is a pretty fine seat, well-wooded [with pubic hair], with a sweet house in the midst of a circle? Say no more.

Sir Petronel's wife, of course, is Gertrude.

Quicksilver continued:

"I wish I were its farmer, for a hundred pounds a year!"

He would rent the land for a hundred pounds, and he could immediately sell the wood for two hundred pounds. He would, no doubt, also plow the "land," and possibly charge others to plow it.

Security said:

"Excellent Master Francis, how I do long to do thee good! How I do hunger and thirst to have the honor to enrich thee!"

Matthew 5:6 states, *Blessed are they which do hunger and thirst after righteousness: for they shall be filled*" (King James Version).

Security continued:

"Aye, even to die, so that thou might inherit my living. Even hunger and thirst! For on my religion, Master Francis — and so tell Knight Petronel — I do it to do him a pleasure."

"By the Virgin Mary, Dad, his horses are now coming up to bear down his lady," Quicksilver said. "Will thou lend him thy stable to set them in?"

"Indeed, Master Francis, I would be loath to lend my stable out of doors — to a stranger," Security said. "In a greater matter I will pleasure him, but not in this."

Frank Quicksilver said to himself:

"A pox on your 'hunger and thirst'!"

He then said out loud:

"Well, Dad, let him have money.

"All he could in any way get is bestowed on a ship now bound for Virginia, the frame of which voyage is so closely conveyed and secretly carried out that neither his new lady nor any of her friends know it.

"Notwithstanding, as soon as his lady's hand is gotten to the sale of her inheritance, and you have furnished him with money, he will immediately hoist sail and go away."

Impoverished gallants sometimes traveled to Virginia to make a new life for themselves.

Security said:

"Now, may a frank — steady — gale of wind go with him, Master Frank! We have too few such knight adventurers. Who would not sell away competent and moderate certainties to purchase, with any danger, excellent uncertainties?"

In other words: Who wouldn't trade away safe and certain money to gamble and risk it all on a dangerous chance of getting an uncertain but excellent profit?

Security wouldn't.

He continued:

"Your true knight venturer always does it. Let his wife seal today; he shall have his money today."

When Sir Petronel's wife put her seal on the contract for the sale of the land, he would get the money.

Quicksilver began:

"Tomorrow she shall, Dad, before she goes into the country; to work her to which action with the more tricky contrivances, I purpose immediately to advance my sweet Sin here to the place of her gentlewoman-attendant; whom you, for the more credibility, shall present as your friend's daughter, a gentlewoman of the country, newly come up to London with a will for a while to learn fashions, indeed, and be in attendance to some lady; and she shall buzz pretty and devious chat into her lady's ear, feeding her humors so serviceably — as you know is the manner of such as she is —"

"Sweet Sin" refers to 1) Sindefy, and 2) the sin of lechery.

Security interrupted, "True, good Master Francis."

Quicksilver finished:

"— so that she shall keep her port — her mind — open to anything she recommends to her."

Sindefy could help convince Gertrude to sell her inheritance.

Security said:

"On my religion, I swear that this is a most fashionable project. As good she spoil the lady as the lady spoil her, for it is three to one of one side."

The word "spoil" can mean 1) plunder, and 2) corrupt her character.

The odds are three to one in favor of Sindefy plundering Gertrude rather than Gertrude corrupting Sindefy's character.

Security continued:

"Sweet Mistress Sin, how you are bound to Master Francis! I do not doubt to see you shortly wed one of the head men of our city."

"Head men" are 1) movers and shakers, and 2) cuckolds, who were supposed to have invisible horns growing on their head.

"But sweet Frank, when shall my father Security present me to Gertrude?" Sindefy asked.

Frank Quicksilver answered, "With all festination and speed. I have broken the ice to it and suggested it to Gertrude already, and I will immediately go to the knight's house, whither, my good old Dad, let me ask thee with all formality to man — to escort — her."

The knight's house was the dwelling where he and Gertrude were staying independently in London.

Security replied:

"Command me, Master Francis; I do hunger and thirst to do thee service."

He then said to Sindefy:

"Come, sweet Mistress Sin, take leave of my Winifred, and we will instantly meet frank Master Francis at your lady's."

Winifred was Security's young wife.

"At your lady's" means the place where Gertrude and Sir Petronel were staying. Once Sindefy gets the place as Gertrude's gentlewoman-attendant, Gertrude will be her lady.

Winifred appeared at a window above them.

She called, "Where is my Cu there? Cu?"

"Cu" was Winifred pet name for Se-CU-rity.

"Cu" is the beginning of the word "Cuckold."

"Aye, Winnie," Security said.

"Will thou come in, sweet Cu?" Winifred asked.

"Aye, Winnie, right now," Security said.

Everyone except Quicksilver exited.

Alone, he said to himself:

"'Aye, Winnie,' said he?

"That's all he can do, poor man; he may well cut off her name at Winnie."

In other words: Winifred can whinny like a mare, but Security cannot perform the services of a stallion to a mare. He is unable to free her from her desire for an orgasm by giving her one.

In this society, "freed" was sometimes spelled "fred."

An old, jealous husband can keep a young wife from having freedom.

An old, jealous, impotent husband can also keep a young wife free of sexual satisfaction. Winni-freed has been freed of whinnying "Oh! Oh! Oh! Oh! Oh!" in bed.

If Security was impotent, he would be forced to say "nay" to any requests for sex.

A synonym of "whinny" is "neigh."

Quicksilver continued:

"Oh, it is an egregious pandar! What won't a usurious knave be, as long as he may be rich? Oh, it is a notable Jew's trump!"

A Jew's trump is a Jew's harp: a term for a usurer.

According to Quicksilver, Security was or would be willing to use his young wife, Winifred, to get wealth from other people.

Quicksilver continued:

"I hope to live to see dog's meat made from the old usurer's flesh, dice made from his bones, and indentures made from his skin; and yet his skin is too thick to make parchment, but it would make good boots for a peterman to catch salmon in."

A peterman is a fisherman. St. Peter was a fisherman. Peter boats were trawlers.

A peterman is also a pandar. The salmon are the peterman's prey. "Boots" can mean "booty" and "plunder." Boots could be the bait for the salmon that the peterman wants to catch.

Quicksilver continued:

"The only smooth skin to make fine vellum — fine, smooth parchment — is a Puritan's skin; they are the smoothest and slickest knaves in a country."

He exited and went to Sir Petronel's lodging.

Sir Petronel, who was wearing riding boots and carrying a riding wand, aka riding crop, talked with Quicksilver. They were at Sir Petronel's lodging.

Sir Petronel said:

"I'll be out of this wicked town as fast as my horse can trot.

"Here's now no good action for a man to spend his time in. Taverns grow dead; ordinaries are blown up and ruined financially and closed down; plays are at a standstill; houses of whore-hospitality are at a fall and in a low state; not a hat-feather is waving nor a spur is jingling anywhere.

"I'll go away immediately."

Frank Quicksilver said, "You'd best take some crowns in your purse, knight, or else your eastward castle will smoke but miserably."

Sir Petronel did not have money to buy firewood.

"Oh, Frank!" Sir Petronel said. "My castle? Alas, all the castles I have are built with air, as thou know."

"I know it, knight, and therefore I wonder to where your lady is going," Quicksilver said.

Sir Petronel replied:

"Indeed, to seek her fortune, I think.

"I said I had a castle and land eastward, and eastward she will go without contradiction; her coach and the coach of the sun must meet full butt."

There was no castle, and so Gertrude would continue to journey eastward until she meets the Sun head-on.

Phoebus Apollo drove the Sun-chariot, aka Sun-coach.

Sir Petronel continued:

"And the sun being outshined with Her Ladyship's glory, she fears he goes westward to hang himself."

The sun, outshone by Gertrude's splendor, will, she imagines, go westward to the gallows at Tyburn and hang itself. Yes, Gertrude is that egotistical.

"And I fear, when her enchanted castle becomes invisible, Her Ladyship will return and follow his example," Quicksilver said.

"Oh, I wish that she would have the grace to hang herself, for I shall never be able to pacify her when she sees herself deceived so," Sir Petronel said.

Quicksilver said:

"Pacifying her can be made to happen as easily as can be.

"Tell her she mistook your directions, and that shortly you yourself will go down with her to show her that your castle exists. And then, just clothe her crupper in a new gown and you may drive her any way you wish."

A "crupper" is a horse's hindquarters, but here it is Gertrude's butt.

Quicksilver continued:

"For these women, sir, are like Essex calves: You must wriggle them on by the tail continually, or they will never drive orderly."

Calves could be made to move in the desired direction by twisting their tails.

Metaphorically, a man who wriggles his wife's tail can make her move in the desired direction. The man must continually satisfy her in bed.

Sir Petronel said, "But alas, sweet Frank, thou know my financial ability and resources will not furnish her blood — her passion and desire — with those costly humors and indulgences."

In other words, he can't afford to buy her expensive items such as new gowns.

"Cast that cost on me, sir," Quicksilver said. "I have spoken to my old pandar, Security, for money or commodity, and commodity, if you are willing, I know he will procure you."

Quicksilver was trying to swindle Sir Petronel by getting him to buy a commodity. Someone who needed money would get a loan, but if that person were desperate or foolish, he could be induced to accept part or all of the loan in the form of shoddy goods of various kinds, such as dolls and hobbyhorses. These would be sold at a loss.

For example, someone would borrow one hundred pounds and would get what was supposed to be one hundred pounds' worth of a commodity. The victim would sell the commodity for fifty pounds but would owe the lender one hundred pounds. The swindle was a way to get around laws limiting the amount of interest that could be demanded for a loan. Often, the man being swindled was a young gallant who consorted with prostitutes.

"Commodity!" Sir Petronel asked. "Alas, what commodity?"

"Why, sir, what do you say to figs and raisins?" Quicksilver asked.

"A plague on figs and raisins and all such frail, easily spoiled commodities!" Sir Petronel said. "We shall make nothing from them."

A "frail" is also a kind of basket in which figs and other fruit can be kept.

"Why, then, sir, what do you say to forty pounds in roasted beef?" Quicksilver said.

"Out upon it, I have less stomach to that than to the figs and raisins," Sir Petronel said. "I'll go out of town, although I sojourn with a friend of mine, for I must not stay here; my creditors have set a watch to arrest me, and I have no friend under heaven but my sword to bail me out."

"Out upon" means 1) "curses upon," or 2) "damnation to," according to the *Oxford English Dictionary*.

He could fight with his sword, or he could hock it to get money for bail.

For a knight to be without a sword was a disgrace.

Frank Quicksilver said, "God save me, knight, put them in sufficient sureties — securities — rather than let your sword bail you. Let them take their choice, either the King's Bench or the Fleet, or which of the two Counters they like best, for, by the Lord, I like none of them."

Counters are prisons, as are the King's Bench and the Fleet. One sufficient surety was to allow them to know that the debtor, Sir Petronel, was securely imprisoned.

Another kind of sufficient surety was to give them secure guarantees that they would be paid. Since Sir Petronel had no money, the guarantees would have to be made by someone else.

"Well, Frank, there is no jesting with my earnest necessity," Sir Petronel said. "Thou know if I don't get ready money immediately to further my voyage begun, all's lost, and all is lost that I have already paid out about it."

"Earnest" is money paid in advance to secure a contract.

"Ready money" is cash.

"Why, then, sir, in earnest: If you can get your wise lady to set her hand to the sale of her inheritance, the bloodhound Security will smell out ready money for you instantly," Quicksilver said.

Sir Petronel said:

"There spoke an angel!"

One kind of angel is the coin called an angel.

Sir Petronel continued:

"To bring her to which conformity, I must feign myself extremely amorous, and, alleging urgent excuses for my stay behind, part with her as passionately as she would from her foisting — farting, stinking — hound."

Quicksilver said:

"You have the sow by the right ear, sir. That's the right way to proceed.

"I warrant there was never a child who longed more to ride a cockhorse or wear his new coat than she longs to ride in her new coach. She would long for everything when she was a maiden, and now she will run mad for them. I lay my life she will have four children every year; and what charge and change — expense and inconstancy — of humor you must endure while she is pregnant with child, and how she will tie you to your tackling until she is with child, a dog would not endure."

The word "tackle" can mean "genitals." Gertrude will keep her husband, Sir Petronel, very busy in bed until she becomes pregnant.

Quicksilver continued:

"Nay, there is no turnspit dog bound to his wheel more servilely than you shall be to her wheel."

Wheels are circles, and women have sexual circles.

Quicksilver continued:

"For as that dog can never climb the top of his turnspit except when the top comes under him, so shall you never climb the top of her contentment but when she is under you."

Dogs walked in exercise wheels to turn the spit on which food was roasted. The dog will never reach the top of the wheel, except when the wheel revolves and the top goes under its paws.

Because of his lack of money, Sir Petronel will never be able to satisfy Gertrude's desires, except when she is under him during sex.

"By God's light, how thou terrify me!" Sir Petronel said.

Quicksilver said:

"Nay, pay attention, sir.

"What nurses, what midwives, what fools, what physicians, what cunning women [fortune tellers and diviners] must be sought for — fearing sometimes she is bewitched, sometimes in a consumption — to tell her tales, to talk bawdy to her, to make her laugh, to give her glisters [enemas], to let her blood under the tongue and between the toes —"

Bloodletting took place in various parts of the body, including under the tongue and in the foot.

Quicksilver continued:

"— how she will revile and kiss you, spit in your face and lick it off again; how she will boast that you are her creature, that she made you out of nothing; how she could have had thousand-mark jointures [thousand-coin marriage settlements]; she could have been made a lady by a Scotch knight and never have married him —"

She could have been a Scotch knight's common-law wife.

A jointure is joint wealth owned both by a husband and a wife. If the husband dies first, the wife will own the wealth and be provided for.

King James I of England was also King James VI of Scotland. He sold knighthoods to raise money.

Quicksilver continued:

"— she could have had poignados in her bed every morning —"

An alternate form of "poignado" is "poinado."

Perhaps "poignado" is a portmanteau word combining "poinado" and "panada" and "poignant."

Panadas are bread puddings, and poinados are small daggers.

In this context, a small dagger is metaphorically a penis.

In this society, "poignant" refers to sharpness of mental and physical feelings. It also refers to sharp, pungent tastes. Gertrude has a sharp desire for bread puddings and for sex.

A proverb stated, "Puddings and paramours would be hotly handled."

Quicksilver continued:

"— how she set you up, and how she will pull you down — you'll never be able to stand upon your legs to endure it."

"How she set you up" means 1) how she set you up financially, or 2) how she gave you an erection.

"Pull you down" means 1) ruin you financially, or 2) make you no longer have an erection.

The word "stand" is slang for "erection." Because of sexual exhaustion, Sir Petronel will not be able to maintain an erection.

Sir Petronel said:

"Out of my fortune, what a death is my life bound face-to-face to!

"The best thing about it is that a large, time-fitted, opportunistic conscience is bound to nothing. Marriage is just a form in the school of policy and cunning deception, to which scholars sit fastened only with painted — imaginary — chains.

"Old Security's young wife is never the further off with me. She is still accessible to me."

Books were valuable and were sometimes chained to desks or tables, but scholars, who were supposed to be "tied" to their desks, could move around as desired.

Sir Petronel was saying that an unscrupulous man could get out of marriage ties, and he was saying that although old Security's young wife was married, he could still try to seduce her.

Quicksilver said, "Thereby lies a tale, sir. The old usurer will be here immediately with my punk Sindefy, whom you know your lady has promised me to employ for her gentlewoman-attendant, and he — with a purpose to feed on you — invites you most solemnly by me to supper."

Sir Petronel said:

"It falls out excellently fitly.

"I see desire of gain makes jealousy venturous and willing to take risks."

Seeing Gertrude coming toward them, Sir Petronel said, "See, Frank, here comes my lady. Lord, how she views thee! She does not know thee, I think. She doesn't recognize you in this bravery — this splendid clothing you are wearing."

Gertrude asked:

"How are things now?"

She then asked Quicksilver:

"Who are you, I ask?"

He answered, "One Master Francis Quicksilver, if it shall please Your Ladyship."

Of course, she recognized the name.

Gertrude said to herself:

"God's my dignity! As I am a lady, if he did not make me blush so that my eyes stood a-watering! I wish that I were unmarried again."

She was impressed by his fine clothing.

She then asked out loud:

"Where's the woman I am going to employ as my gentlewoman-attendant, I ask?"

Security and Sindefy entered the scene.

"See, madam, she now comes to attend you," Quicksilver said.

Security said, "God save my honorable knight and his worshipful lady!"

He removed his hat and bowed.

"You're very welcome," Gertrude said. "You must not put on your hat yet."

Normally, after bowing, a man would be invited to put on his hat again.

"Madam, until I know Your Ladyship's further pleasure, I will not presume to put on my hat again," Security said.

"And is this a gentleman's daughter newly come out of the country?" Gertrude asked about Sindefy.

"She is, madam," Security said, "and she is one whom her father has a special care to bestow in some honorable lady's service, to put her out of her honest humors and chaste whims, indeed, for she had a great desire to be a nun, if it shall please you."

The word "nun" was sometimes used to mean "whore."

"A nun?" Gertrude asked. "What nun? A nun substantive or a nun adjective?"

She had misunderstood. She was talking about kinds of nouns, not nuns.

William Lily wrote in his *An Introduction of the Eight Parts of Speech* (London, 1544), "A noun substantive is that standeth by himself and requireth not another word to be joined with him [...]. A noun adjective [i.e. an adjective] is that [...] requireth to be joined with another word."

"A nun substantive, madam, I hope, if a nun be a noun," Security said. "But I mean, lady, a vowed maid of that order."

Of course, "vowed" sounds much like "vowel."

A "maid" is a maiden.

The word "substantive" means "noun" in the sense of "person, place, or thing."

A substantive nun is a real (religious) nun.

An adjectival nun is a whore who needs to be joined with another "word": a man.

Gertrude said, "I'll teach her to be a maid of the order, I promise you."

Gertrude being Gertrude, a "maid of the order" is a sexual initiate.

She then asked Sindefy, "And can you do any work that belongs to a lady's chamber?"

"What I cannot do, madam, I would be glad to learn," Sindefy replied.

Gertrude said:

"Well said. Hold up, then; hold up your head, I say."

Sindefy had been keeping her head bowed as she talked to Gertrude.

Gertrude then said to her:

"Come here a little closer."

"I thank Your Ladyship," Sindefy said.

Gertrude added:

"And listen —"

She said to Security:

"Good man, you may put on your hat now. I am not looking at you."

She then said to Sindefy:

"I must have you one of my faction now, not of my knight's, maid."

Gertrude wanted to be the boss in her home, not Sir Petronel. She therefore wanted all the servants to be on her side and obey her orders. She wanted them to be in her bow — that is, under her control.

"No, indeed, madam, of yours," Sindefy said.

Her words were ambiguous. They could mean 1) No, I will not be of your faction: I will be of your husband's faction, or) No, I will not be of your husband's faction: I will be of your faction.

Gertrude continued:

"And you must draw all my servants in my bow, and keep my counsel, and tell me tales, and put riddles to me, and read on a book sometimes when I am busy [ahem, busy in bed, perhaps not with her husband], and laugh at country gentlewomen, and command anything in the house for my retainers, and care not what you spend, for it is all mine."

When Gertrude wanted to commit adultery, she would have Sindefy read a book instead of act as her chaperone.

Gertrude was claiming that all the wealth would be hers, although in a patriarchal society, all the wealth would normally be the husband's. Since her husband, Sir Petronel, was in fact impoverished, although Gertrude did not know that yet, all the wealth would in fact be hers.

Gertrude continued:

"And in any case you must be still and always a maiden, whatsoever you do, or whatsoever any man can do to you."

"I warrant Your Ladyship for that," Security said.

Yes, Sindefy would call herself a maiden, aka virgin. It did not matter that she wasn't one.

Gertrude said to Sindefy:

"Very well. You shall ride in my coach with me into the country tomorrow morning."

She then said to her husband:

"Come, knight, please let's make a short supper, and go to bed quickly."

"Nay, good madam," Security said. "This night I have a short supper at home that waits on His Worship's acceptation."

He wanted Sir Petronel to be his supper guest.

"By my faith, but he shall not go, sir," Gertrude said. "I shall swoon and faint if he eats a meal away from me."

"Please, let me go to the supper," her husband, Sir Petronel, said. "Shall Security lose his provision — shall he lose what he has spent on this meal?"

"Aye, by our Lady, sir, rather than I lose my longing," Gertrude said.

Her longing was to have sex with her husband.

Gertrude continued:

"Come in, I say. As I am a lady, you shall not go!"

Quicksilver whispered to Security, "I told him what a burr he had gotten."

Gretchen was sticking to Sir Petronel like a burr.

According to the *Oxford English Dictionary*, a burr can also be 1) "a circle," or 2) "A broad iron ring on a tilting spear just behind the place for the hand."

A burr can be a vagina (1 above), and it can be a vagina enveloping a penis (2 above: a ring on a spear).

"If you will not sup away from your knight, madam, let me entreat Your Ladyship to sup at my house with him," Security said.

"No, by my faith, sir," Gertrude said, "because then we cannot be in bed soon enough after supper."

Sir Petronel said:

"What a medicine is this!"

He meant: What a bitter pill is this!

He continued:

"Well, Master Security, you are newly married as well as I; I hope you are bound as well. We must honor our young wives, you know."

Quicksilver whispered to Security, "Honor her wish in policy, Dad, until tomorrow she has sealed the contract and signed away her land."

He meant that Sir Petronel ought to obey the wishes of his wife until she had signed away her property. This was "policy": something that needed to be done in order to plunder her wealth.

"I hope in the morning your knighthood will yet breakfast with me?" Security asked.

"As early as you will, sir," Sir Petronel said.

"I thank Your good Worship," Security said. "I do hunger and thirst to do you good, sir."

"Come, sweet knight, come," Gertrude said. "I do hunger and thirst to be in bed with thee."

They exited.

CHAPTER 3

— 3.1 —

Sir Petronel, Quicksilver, Security, Bramble, and Winifred met together at Security's house. They had just eaten breakfast.

Bramble was a lawyer.

"Thanks for our feast-like breakfast, good Master Security," Sir Petronel said. "I am sorry by reason of my immediate haste to go on so long a voyage to Virginia, I am without means to make any kind amends and requitals to show how affectionately I take your kindness, and to confirm by some worthy ceremony a perpetual league of friendship between us."

He lacked money to perform some action that would repay Security for the meal.

Security replied:

"Excellent knight, let this be a token between us of inviolable friendship.

"I am newly married to this fair gentlewoman, you know, and, by my hope to make her fruitful and pregnant, although I am something in years, I vow faithfully to you to make you godfather, although in your absence, to the first child I am blessed with. And henceforth call me gossip, I ask you, if you please to accept it."

A godfather will try to encourage the child to develop in a wholesome way, something that can be difficult when the two are separated by a great distance, especially in the early 1600s.

In this society, a gossip is a friend.

Sir Petronel said:

"In the highest degree of gratitude, my most worthy gossip.

"For confirmation of which friendly title, let me entreat my fair gossip, your wife here, to accept this diamond and keep it as my gift to her first child, wheresoever my fortune in the outcome of my voyage shall bestow me."

He offered Winifred a diamond ring.

Godparents traditionally gave silver spoons to the godchild. A ring was an unusual present for a godchild, but rings were usual presents given by lovers.

Security said to Winifred:

"What is this now, my coy wedlock — my shy wife. Why are you reluctant to accept so noble a favor and gift?

"Take it, I tell you, with all affection, and, by way of taking your leave, present boldly your lips to our honorable gossip."

Winifred accepted the ring.

Quicksilver said to himself, "How venturous he is to him, and how jealous to others!"

Security was usually jealous concerning his wife, but because he was greedy to get the ring and to get Sir Petronel's wife's land, he allowed his wife to kiss Sir Petronel.

Kissing Winifred, Sir Petronel said:

"Long may this kind touch of our lips print in our hearts all the forms of affection!"

One form of affection is sex.

Sir Petronel then said to Security:

"And now, my good gossip, if the written contract is ready to which my wife should seal her name, let them be brought this morning before she takes her coach into the country, and my kindness shall persuade her to dispatch it."

"The written contract is ready, sir," Security said. "My learned counsel here, Master Bramble the lawyer, has perused it, and within this hour I will bring the scrivener — the notary — with it to your worshipful lady."

"Good Master Bramble, I will here take my leave of you, then," Sir Petronel said. "God send you fortunate pleas and lawsuits, sir, and contentious clients!"

"And you foreright — favorable — winds, sir, and a fortunate voyage!" Bramble said.

He exited.

A messenger entered the scene and said, "Sir Petronel, here are three or four gentlemen who desire to speak with you."

"Who are they?" Sir Petronel asked.

"They are your followers — your partners — in this voyage, knight: Captain Seagull and his associates," Quicksilver said. "I met them this morning and told them you would be here."

Sir Petronel said to the messenger:

"I ask you to let them enter."

The messenger exited.

Sir Petronel then said:

"I know they long to be gone, for their stay is dangerous."

If they delayed setting off on their journey, their ship could be seized to pay off debt.

Captain Seagull, Scapethrift, and Spendall entered the scene.

Captain Seagull was the captain of the ship that was supposed to take Sir Petronel to Virginia, and Scapethrift and Spendall were adventurers with Captain Seagull.

"God save my honorable Colonel!" Captain Seagull said.

By "Colonel," he meant Sir Petronel.

"Welcome, good Captain Seagull, and worthy gentlemen!" Sir Petronel replied. "If you will meet my friend Frank here, and me, at the Blue Anchor Tavern by Billingsgate this evening, we will there drink to our happy voyage, be merry, and take boat to our ship with all expedition — with all haste."

"Defer your voyage to Virginia no longer, I ask you, sir," Captain Seagull said, "but as your voyage is hitherto carried closely and secretly and in another knight's name, so for your own safety and ours let the secrecy be continued, our meeting and speedy purpose of departing known to as few as is possible, lest your ship and goods be seized for debt."

"Well advised, Captain," Quicksilver said. "Our colonel shall have money this morning to dispatch all our departures. Bring those gentlemen at night to the place appointed, and with our skins full of vintage — our bellies full of wine — we'll take occasion by the vantage and go away."

They would take opportunity by the forelock — at the opportune, advantageous time — and sail away.

A proverb stated, "Take Time (Occasion, aka Opportunity) by the forelock, for she is bald behind."

"We will not fail to be there, sir," Captain Seagull said.

Sir Petronel replied:

"Good morning, good Captain, and my worthy associates."

He then said to Winifred:

"Health and all sovereignty to my beautiful gossip!"

"Sovereignty" is freedom. An old, jealous husband can keep a young wife from having freedom.

He then said to Security:

"As for you, sir, we shall see you very soon with the written contract."

"With the written contract and crowns — coins, money — for my honorable gossip," Security said. "I do hunger and thirst to do you good, sir!"

Outside the lodging of Sir Petronel and Gertrude, a coachman appeared, in his frock, aka long coat, in haste and eating part of his breakfast.

The coachman said to himself, "Here's a stir when citizens ride out of town, indeed, as if all the house were on fire! By God's light, they will not give a man leave to eat his breakfast before he rises."

Hamlet, a footman, arrived in haste and said, "What, Coachman! My lady's coach, for shame! Her Ladyship's ready to come down."

In Act 4, scene 5, of *Hamlet*, Ophelia calls for her coach. In *Hamlet*, she goes mad, and Gertrude's desire to be a lady can be regarded as a kind of madness.

The coachman exited.

Potkin, a tankard bearer, entered the scene and said:

"By God's foot, Hamlet, are you mad? To where do you run now? You should brush up my old mistress!"

Part of Hamlet's job was to brush Mrs. Touchstone's fine clothing.

Hamlet exited.

Sindefy entered the scene and said, "What, Potkin! You must put away your tankard and put on your blue coat and wait upon Mistress Touchstone as she goes into the country."

A blue coat was part of a serving man's livery: his distinctive clothing.

Mistress Touchstone was Mrs. Touchstone. She was going with her daughter Gertrude into the countryside.

Sindefy exited.

Potkin said to himself, "I will, indeed, right away."

He exited.

Gertrude and her mother were only two people, but they kept many servants hopping.

Mistress Fond and Mistress Gazer entered the scene. They were city wives: female citizens of London. They had urban tastes and manners. They were not lower class, nor were they the highest class. They were a middling class.

"Come, sweet Mistress Gazer, let's watch here and see my Lady Flash take coach."

Lady Flash was Mrs. Petronel Flash: Gertrude.

"On my word, here's a very fine place to stand in," Mistress Gazer said. "Did you see the new ship launched yesterday, Mistress Fond?"

"Oh, God, and we citizens should lose such a sight!" Mistress Fond said.

"I promise, here will be double as many people to see her take coach as there were to see the new ship take water," Mistress Gazer said.

"Take water" is ambiguous. "Take to water" meant that the ship was launched. "Take on water" meant that the ship was sinking or that the ship was bringing on board supplies of fresh water.

Gertrude thought that her ship of fortune had arrived, but readers know that her husband is impoverished.

"Oh, she's married to a very fine castle in the country, they say," Mistress Fond said.

Gertrude thought that she had married money and property and wealth.

"But there are no giants in the castle, are there?" Mistress Gazer asked.

"Oh, no, they say her knight killed them all, and therefore he was knighted," Mistress Fond said.

Giants are just as real as Sir Petronel's castle.

"I wish to God Her Ladyship would come away — would make her appearance!" Mistress Gazer said.

Gertrude, Mistress Touchstone, Sindefy, Hamlet, and Potkin entered the scene.

"She comes! She comes! She comes!" Mistress Fond said.

"Pray heaven bless Your Ladyship!" Mistress Gazer and Mistress Fond said.

"Thank you, good people," Gertrude said.

Queen Elisabeth I often said these words when addressing the public.

"My coach, for the love of heaven, my coach!" Gertrude said. "In good truth, I shall swoon and faint else."

"Coach! Coach!" Hamlet called. "My lady's coach!"

He exited.

Gertrude said:

"As I am a lady, I think I am with child already, I long for a coach so."

A pregnant woman often has cravings for strange combinations of food; Gertrude had a craving to ride in a coach.

Gertrude then asked:

"May one be with child before they are married, mother?"

Her mother, Mrs. Touchstone, answered, "Aye, by our lady, madam, a little thing does that. I have seen a little prick no bigger than a pin's head swell bigger and bigger until it has come to an ancome, and even so it is in these cases."

A tiny pinprick in the skin can swell up and become an ulcerous boil, aka an ancome.

A little prick can swell up, enter a vagina, and cause a woman's belly to swell up.

The word "case" can mean "vagina."

Hamlet returned and said, "Your coach is coming, madam."

Gertrude said:

"That's well done and well said. Now, heaven! I think I am even up to the knees in preferment."

"Preferment" is promotion to high rank.

She sang:

"*But a little higher, but a little higher, but a little higher,*

"*There, there, there lies Cupid's fire.*"

Yes, Cupid's fire lies a little higher than a woman's knees. It's up there by the pubic bone. It's the vagina.

The song lines are from Thomas Campion's bawdy song "Beauty, Since You So Much Desire" from his *Fourth Book of Airs* (1617), in which he refers to toes and heels and then to Cupid's fire.

"But must this young man, if it shall please you, madam, run by your coach all the way on foot?" Mrs. Touchstone asked.

Footmen ran beside a coach as it traveled. They were servants to the high-class people riding inside the coach.

Gertrude's footman was Hamlet.

"Aye, by my faith, I warrant him," Gertrude said. "He gives no other milk, as I have another servant who does."

"No other milk" can metaphorically mean "no other duty."

Milk is a whitish fluid; so is semen.

A servant can be 1) an employee, or 2) a lover.

Mrs. Touchstone said:

"Alas! It is even a pity, I think. For God's sake, madam, buy him but a hobby-horse; let the poor youth have something between his legs to ease them."

A hobby-horse can be 1) a child's toy horse: a stick with a horse's head on one end, or 2) a whore.

Yes, youths do have a thing between their legs. Yes, that thing can be eased with one kind of hobby-horse.

Mrs. Touchstone continued:

"Alas, we must do as we would be done to."

The verb "do" can mean "to have sex with."

The Golden Rule is to treat other people as you would like to be treated.

Matthew 7:12 states, "*Therefore all things whatsoever ye would that men should do to you: do ye even so to them: for this is the law and the prophets*" (King James Version).

If you would like other people to have sex with you, then you ought to have sex with other people.

"Bah, hold your peace, dame," Gertrude said. "You talk like an old fool, I tell you."

Sir Petronel and Quicksilver entered the scene.

"Will thou be gone, sweet honeysuckle, before I can go with thee?" Sir Petronel asked.

"I request of thee, sweet knight, let me," Gertrude said. "I do so long to dress up thy castle before thou come. But I marvel how my modest sister occupies herself this morning, that she cannot wait on me as I go to my coach as well as her mother."

"By the Virgin Mary, madam, she's married by this time to apprentice Golding," Quicksilver said. "Your father, and someone more, stole to church with them in all haste, so that the cold meat and food left at your wedding might serve to furnish their nuptial table."

Gertrude said:

"There's no base fellow, my father, now, but he's even fit to father such a daughter. He must call me daughter no more now, but 'madam,' and 'please you, madam,' and 'please Your Worship, madam,' indeed.

"Out upon him! Marry his daughter to a base apprentice!"

Golding was no longer an apprentice, but Gretchen did not know that.

Mrs. Touchstone asked:

"What should one do? Is there no law for one who marries a woman's daughter against her — that is, my — will?"

Mr. Touchstone had gotten their daughter Mildred married to a man whom Mrs. Touchstone did not want her married to.

Mrs. Touchstone then asked:

"How shall we punish him, madam?"

Gertrude said:

"As I am a lady, if it would snow, we'd so pebble them with snowballs as they come from church!"

She wanted to pebble with snowballs her sister, Mildred, too.

Gertrude continued:

"But sirrah, Frank Quicksilver —"

"Aye, madam," Quicksilver said.

"Do thou remember since thou and I clapped what-d'ye-call'ts in the garret?" Gertrude asked.

They had clapped genitals — bumped uglies — together.

"I don't know what you mean, madam," Quicksilver replied.

It was best not to acknowledge that he had had sex with Gertrude.

Gertrude sang:

"*His head as white as milk,*

"*All flaxen was his hair;*

"*But now he is dead,*

"*And laid in his bed,*

"*And never will come again.*

"God be at your labor!"

The color of flax is pale yellowish-grey.

Milk is a whitish fluid.

The word "head" can mean 1) the froth at the top of a glass of beer, and 2) the cream that rises to the top of unhomogenized milk.

"His head as white as milk" may mean "semen."

Quicksilver would never come — ejaculate — with her again.

Touchstone, Golding, and Mildred entered the scene. Mildred was carrying rosemary, which represents constancy and loyalty.

"Was there ever such a lady as Gertrude?" Sir Petronel quietly asked himself.

"See, madam, the bride and bridegroom!" Quicksilver said.

Gertrude said:

"God's my precious!"

This oath may mean 1) By God's precious blood, or 2) God's my precious one.

Gertrude continued:

"God give you joy, Mistress What-lack-you!"

"What lack you" is the cry of a business person selling wares. Gertrude's "Mistress What-lack-you!" meant "Mrs. Tradesman's Wife."

Gertrude continued:

"Now out upon thee, baggage, my sister married in a taffeta hat?"

One definition of "baggage "is a worthless woman.

Gertrude preferred hats that were fancier than taffeta hats.

Gertrude continued:

"By the Virgin Mary, hang you!

"Westward with a wanion — a vengeance, aka curse — to ye! Nay, I have done with ye, minion, then, truly."

A minion can be 1) a hussy, or 2) a darling.

Mildred was her father's favorite daughter.

Gertrude continued:

"Never look to have my countenance — my good will and favor — any more, nor never look to have anything I can do for thee.

"Thou ride in my coach? Or come down to my castle? Fie upon thee! I charge thee in My Ladyship's name, call me sister no more."

Touchstone said:

"If it shall please Your Worship, this is not your sister. This is my daughter, and she calls me father, and so does not Your Ladyship, if it shall please Your Worship, madam."

He disliked his daughter Gertrude's pride.

Mrs. Touchstone said:

"No, and Gertrude must not call thee father by the practice of heraldry because thou make thy apprentice thy son as well as she your prodigy."

She then said to Golding:

"Ah, thou misproud — wrongfully proud — apprentice, do thou dare presume to marry a lady's sister?"

Golding answered:

"It pleased my master, indeed, to embolden me with his favor.

"And although I confess myself far unworthy so worthy a wife (being in part her servant, as I am your apprentice) yet (since I may say it without boasting) I am born a gentleman, and by the trade I have learned from my master (which I trust taints not my blood) able with my own industry and portion to maintain your daughter, my hope is, heaven will so bless our humble beginning that in the end I shall be no disgrace to the grace with which my master has bound me his double apprentice."

"Double apprentice" means 1) apprentice, and 2) son-in-law.

"'Master' me no more, son, if thou think me worthy to be thy father," Touchstone said. "Don't call me 'master.'"

Gertrude said, "'Son'! Now, good lord, how he shines, if you mark him! He's a gentleman!"

"Aye, indeed, madam, I am a gentleman born," Golding said.

"Never stand on your gentry, master bridegroom," Sir Petronel said. "If your legs are no better than your arms, you'll be able to stand upon neither shortly."

He was punning on "coat of arms."

"If it shall please Your good Worship, sir, there are two sorts of gentlemen," Touchstone said.

"What do you mean, sir?" Sir Petronel asked.

Touchstone said, "I make bold to take off my hat to Your Worship —"

"Nay, please don't take off your hat, sir," Sir Petronel said. "Put it on again and then continue with your description of two sorts of gentlemen."

Sir Petronel did not want to put on airs over Touchstone, his father-in-law. Touchstone said:

"If Your Worship will have it so, I say there are two sorts of gentlemen.

"There is a gentleman artificial, and a gentleman natural.

"Now, although Your Worship is a gentleman natural — Work upon that, now!"

The word "natural" can mean 1) by birth, 2) by nature, and/or 3) foolish.

People could artificially raise themselves to a higher social class by 1) acquiring land, and/or 2) acquiring a university degree, and/or 3) acquiring a military commission, and/or 4) practicing law or medicine.

According to the *Oxford English Dictionary*, a gentleman is 1) "A man of high social status," and/or 2) "A man having the characteristics traditionally associated with high social standing; a chivalrous, courteous, or honourable man.”

Quicksilver said:

“Well said and well done, old Touchstone. I am proud to hear thee enter a set speech, indeed.

“Continue, I request thee.”

“I beg your pardon, sir,” Touchstone said. “Your Worship’s a gentleman I do not know. If you are one of my acquaintance, you’re very much disguised, sir.”

The clause “Your Worship’s a gentleman I do not know” can mean “I do not know that Your Worship is a gentleman.”

Touchstone was pretending not to recognize Quicksilver.

“Get on with it, old quipper!” Quicksilver said. “Continue with thy speech, I say.”

Touchstone said:

“What, sir, my speeches were always in vain to Your gracious Worship, and therefore until I speak to you with true, not mock, gallantry indeed, I will save my breath to cool my broth from now on.”

His words showed that he had recognized Quicksilver.

Touchstone then said to Golding and Mildred:

“Come, my ‘poor’ son and daughter, let us hide ourselves in our poor humility and live safe. Ambition consumes itself with the very show.”

He then said to everyone:

“Work upon that now!”

Touchstone, Golding, and Mildred exited.

Gertrude said:

“Let him go, let him go, for God’s sake. Let him make his apprentice his son, for God’s sake; give away his daughter, for God’s sake; and when they come begging to us, for God’s sake, let’s laugh at their ‘good husbandry,’ for God’s sake!”

“Good husbandry” is careful thrift, something that Gertrude did not value.

Gertrude continued:

“Farewell, sweet knight; please make haste to come after me.”

“What shall I say?” Sir Petronel said. “I would not have thee go.”

If she did not go, she would not find out that his castle did not exist.

Quicksilver sang:

"Now, Oh, now, I must depart;
"Parting though it absence move."
He then said:
"This ditty, knight, do I see in thy looks in capital letters — prominently."
He then sang:
"What a grief 'tis to depart,
"And leave the flower that has my heart!
"My sweet lady, and alack for woe,
"Why should we part so?"
He then said:
"Tell truth, knight, and shame all dissembling lovers: Does not your pain lie on that side? Aren't you in pain because you have to leave your wife?"

The pain in the side was his wife. God removed a rib from Adam in order to create Eve.

Genesis 2:22 states, *"And the rib, which the LORD God had taken from man, made he a woman, and brought her unto the man"* (King James Version).

"If it do, can thou tell me how I may cure it?" Sir Petronel asked.

Quicksilver said:

"Excellently easily: Divide yourself in two halves, just by the girdlestead — the waist; send one half with your lady, and keep the other half for yourself."

Taking Gertrude's sexual desires into consideration, Sir Petronel would keep the half that eats. Gretchen would keep the other half: the half that —.

Quicksilver continued:

"Or else do as all true lovers do: Part with your heart and leave your body behind.

"I have seen it done a hundred times. It is as easy a matter for a lover to part without a heart from his sweetheart, and he be never the worse, as for a mouse to get away from a trap and leave his tail behind him.

"Look, here comes the writing: the document."

Security and a scrivener entered the scene.

"Good morning to My worshipful Lady!" Security said. "I present Your Ladyship with this writing, to which if you please to set your hand, with your knight's, a velvet gown shall attend your journey, on my credit."

"What writing is it, knight?" Gertrude asked.

Sir Petronel answered, "The sale, sweetheart, of the poor tenement — poor property — I told thee about, only to make a little money to send thee down furniture for my castle, to which my hand shall lead thee."

He signed the bond first.

"Very well. Now give me your pen, please," Gertrude said.

She signed the bond.

Her inheritance of land had been sold for ready money.

"It goes down without chewing, indeed," Quicksilver said to himself.

She had swallowed the bait of the velvet gown.

"Do Your Worships deliver this as your deed?" the scrivener asked.

"We do," Gertrude and Sir Petronel replied.

"So now, knight, farewell until I see thee," Gertrude said.

"All farewell to my sweetheart!" Sir Petronel replied.

"God be with ye, son knight," Mrs. Touchstone said.

"Farewell, my good mother," Sir Petronel said.

"Farewell, Frank," Gertrude said. "I would eagerly take thee down if I could."

Yes, 1) down in the country, or 2) down in bed so she could change an erection to a non-erection.

Quicksilver said:

"I thank Your good Ladyship."

He then said:

"Farewell, Mistress Sindefy."

Everyone exited except for Petronel, Quicksilver, and Security.

Of course, Gertrude and her mother, Mrs. Touchstone, were going on a journey to see Sir Petronel's nonexistent castle.

"Oh, tedious voyage, whereof there is no end!" Sir Petronel complained. "What will they think of me?"

This kind of voyage is an undertaking; in this particular case, it is a marriage.

Quicksilver replied:

"Think what they wish."

This is ambiguous. It can mean 1) You should think about what they wish, and/or 2) They will think what they wish.

He continued:

"They longed for a vagary — an excursion — into the country, and now they are fitted: They have gotten what they wanted.

"If a woman will marry so she can ride in a coach, she will not care if she rides to her ruin. It is the great end of many of their marriages. This is not the first time a lady has ridden a false journey in her coach, I hope."

Women would often ride in a coach to an assignation, aka a tryst, aka a session of adulterous sex. Or they would sexually ride while in a coach. Adultery often ruined marriages.

Another kind of "false journey" is a wild-goose chase.

Sir Petronel said:

"Nay, it doesn't matter; I care little what they think. He who weighs men's thoughts has his hands full of nothing.

"A man in the course of this world should be like a surgeon's instrument: work in the wounds of others and feel nothing himself. The sharper and subtler, the better."

"As it falls out now, knight, you shall not need to devise excuses or endure her outcries when she returns," Quicksilver said. "We shall before they return be gone where they cannot reach us."

Sir Petronel said to Security, "Well, my kind compeer and associate, you have now the assurance we both can make you. Let me now entreat you that the money we agreed on may be brought to the Blue Anchor Tavern nearby Billingsgate by six o'clock, where I and my chief friends, bound for this voyage, will with feasts attend you."

"The money, my most honorable compeer, shall without fail observe your appointed hour," Security said.

Sir Petronel said:

"Thanks, my dear gossip.

"I must now impart to your approved — attested and proven — love a loving secret, as one on whom my life does more rely in friendly trust than any man alive.

"Nor shall you be the chosen secretary, aka confidant, of my affections for affection only. For I protest (if God bless my return) to make you partner in my action's — my deed's — gain as deeply as if you had ventured with me half my expenses."

If Security had risked with Sir Petronel half of Sir Petronel's expenses, he would lose all that money. If he becomes partner in Sir Petronel's new action or deed, we can expect Security to lose something.

Sir Petronel continued:

"Know then, honest gossip, I have enjoyed with such divine contentment the bed and sexual favors of a gentlewoman whom you well know, with the result that I shall never enjoy this tedious voyage, nor live the least part of the time it requires, without her presence, so much do I thirst and hunger to taste the dear feast of her company.

"And if the hunger and the thirst you vow as my sworn gossip to my wished good is — as I know it is — unfeigned and firm, do me an easy favor in your power."

Security replied:

"Be sure, brave gossip, all that I can do, to my best nerve and utmost strength, is wholly at your service.

"Who is the woman, first, who is your friend?"

A "friend" can be a lover.

Sir Petronel answered:

"The woman is your learned counsel's wife: the wife of the lawyer, Master Bramble, whom I want you to bring out this evening, in honest neighborliness, to take his leave with you of me, your gossip.

"I, in the meantime, will send this my friend — Quicksilver — home to his house, to bring Bramble's wife disguised before his face into our company.

"For love has made her look for such a wile — a devious stratagem — to free her from his tyrannous jealousy, and I would take this course before another, in stealing her away to make us sport and entertainment and fool his circumspection and deceive his watchfulness the more grossly.

"And I am sure that no man like yourself has credit with him to entice his jealous disposition to so long stay abroad and away from his home as may give time to her enlargement and liberation in such safe disguise."

Security said:

"This is a pretty, pithy and vigorous, and most pleasant project and scheme!

"Who would not strain a point of neighborliness for such a point-device — such a perfect plot and plot of vice — that, just as the ship of famous Draco —

Sir Francis Drake — circumnavigated the world in 1580, will wind about the lawyer, compassing the world himself?"

Sir Francis Drake sailed around the world, and now this plot will wind around and bind the lawyer, just as the lawyer's legal papers wind around and bind his victims.

The lawyer Bramble compasses the world: He machinates (engages in plots and schemes), and he manipulates those in his world to his benefit.

Besides "machinate" and "manipulate," the verb "compass" also means 1) to compost, or 2) to manure.

Literally, in a garden, this can be a good thing. But figuratively, Bramble spreads manure around in his world, and it is a bad thing.

Security said:

"He has the world in his arms, and that's enough for him without his wife.

"A lawyer is ambitious, and his head cannot be praised nor raised too high with any fork of highest knavery.

"I'll go fetch him straightaway."

In this society, forks could have two, three, or four prongs. A two-pronged fork can resemble horns — either the horns of the Devil, or the horns of a cuckold.

Security exited.

Sir Petronel said:

"Good, good.

"Now, Frank, go thou home to Security's house, instead of his lawyer's, and bring his wife here.

"She, just like the lawyer's wife, is imprisoned by his stern, usurious jealousy, which could never be overreached thus but with overreaching — that is, be outwitted thus but with trickery."

Security returned and said:

"And, Master Francis, watch for the instant time to enter with his exit — be on watch to enter the house as soon as Bramble exits.

"It will be rare: two fine horned beasts, a camel and a lawyer!"

According to Security, the lawyer would wear the horns of a cuckold: a man with an unfaithful wife.

According to a fable by Aesop, a camel envied the horns of a bull, and asked Jupiter to give him horns. A capricious god, Jupiter not only did not give the camel horns, but also made the camel's ears shorter.

The camel wanted horns but did not get them. According to Security, Bramble does not want horns, but he will get them.

Security exited.

"How the old villain takes joy in practicing villainy!" Quicksilver said.

Security returned and said to Quicksilver:

"And listen, gossip, when you have her here, have your boat ready; ship her to your ship with utmost haste, lest Master Bramble delay you.

"To overreach — surpass — that head that outreaches all heads, it is a trick rampant and high-spirited, it is a very quiblin — a true trick!

"I hope this harvest to pitch cart with lawyers — their heads will be so forked."

Security was saying that instead of using pitchforks to pitch hay into wagons, people could use the forked heads of lawyers to do that.

Security continued:

"This sly touch will get apes — imitators — to invent a number of such tricks."

He exited.

Quicksilver said:

"Was any rascal ever so honied with poison? He delights in a trick that will end up hurting him.

"He who delights in slavish, base avarice is apt to take joy in every sort of vice.

"Well, I'll go fetch his wife, while he fetches the lawyer."

He started to leave, but Sir Petronel said, "But wait, Frank, let's think about how we may disguise her upon this sudden need to do that."

Quicksilver said:

"God's me, there's the mischief!"

"God's me" means "God s' me," aka "God save me" — a strange oath to make when planning to help someone run away with another man's wife.

Or perhaps it means "God is me." Some of these people are trying to act as supreme beings.

He continued:

"But pay attention, here's an excellent trick. Before God, it's a rare and splendid one: I will carry to her a sailor's gown and cap and cover her, and a player's beard."

"Cover her" can mean "have sex with her." Literally, it refers to a stallion covering a mare.

A "player's beard" is an actor's false beard.

It is also an adulterer's pubic hair: something that Quicksilver wished to cover — with his body.

Think of Chaucer's "Miller's Tale" when Absolon encounters a beard after asking for a goodnight kiss.

"And what will you put upon her head?" Sir Petronel asked.

Quicksilver replied, "I told you, a sailor's cap. By God's light, God forgive me, but what kind of figent — fidgety and short — memory do you have?"

"Nay, then, what kind of figent wit have thou?" Sir Petronel asked. "A sailor's cap? How shall she take it off when thou present her to our company?"

"Tush, man, as for that, make her a saucy sailor," Quicksilver said.

"Tush, tush, it is no fit sauce — no fit disguise — for such sweet mutton," Sir Petronel said. "I don't know what to advise."

A proverb stated, "Sweet meat must have sour sauce."

"Mutton" is a word for a prostitute.

Security returned, carrying his wife's good gown, and said, "Knight, knight, here is a rare and splendid trick!"

Sir Petronel said to himself, "By God's wounds, here he is yet again!"

"What stratagem have you now?" Quicksilver asked.

"The best stratagem that ever was," Security said. "You talked of disguising?"

"Aye, by the Virgin Mary, gossip, that's our present care and concern," Sir Petronel said.

Security said:

"Cast care away, then. Cast aside your worries.

"Here's the best trick for plain Security — for I am no better — I think that ever lived.

"Here's my wife's gown, which you may put upon the lawyer's wife, and which I brought you, sir, for two great reasons:

"One reason is, that Master Bramble may take hold of some suspicion that it is my wife and gird me — make fun of me — so, perhaps, with his law wit.

"The other reason (which is cunning policy and trickery indeed) is that my wife may now be tied at home, having no more but her old gown to go abroad outside, and she will not show me a quirk while I firk others — she won't be able to trick me while I trick others.

"Isn't this trick splendid?"

"The best that ever was!" Sir Petronel and Quicksilver said.

"Am I not born to furnish and provide for gentlemen?" Security asked.

He was acting as a pandar to Sir Petronel.

"O my dear gossip!" Sir Petronel said.

Security said:

"Well, wait, Master Francis. Watch for when the lawyer's out, and put it in."

Hmm. "Put it in." Say no more.

But Security meant for Quicksilver to take the dress in to Bramble's wife.

Security continued:

"And now I will go and fetch Bramble."

He started to exit but hesitated.

Quicksilver said:

"O my Dad!"

He then whispered to Sir Petronel:

"He goes as if he were the Devil to fetch the lawyer; and devil shall he be, if horns will make him one."

In medieval stories, the Devil sometimes carried a lawyer to Hell.

Sir Petronel asked Security, "Why, how are things now, gossip? Why do you stay there musing?"

"A toy, a toy runs in my head, indeed," Security said.

A toy is an odd notion or a trick.

Quicksilver said to himself, "A pox on that head! Are there more toys yet?"

"What is it, I ask thee, gossip?" Sir Petronel asked.

"Why, sir, what if you should slip away now with my wife's best gown, with me having no security for it?" Security asked.

He had no guarantee — and no security deposit — that the gown would be returned.

"As for that, I hope, Dad, you will take our words," Quicksilver said.

Security said sarcastically:

"Aye, by the Mass, your word! That's a proper staff for wise Security to lean upon!"

He then said:

"But it does not matter. For once I'll entrust my name to your cracked, unsound credits; let it take no shame.

"Fetch the wench, Frank."

Frank Quicksilver said:

"I'll wait upon you, sir —"

Security exited.

Quicksilver continued:

"— and fetch you over in such a way that you were never so fetched. Yes, I will deceive as you have never been deceived before."

He then said to Sir Petronel:

"Go to the tavern, knight; your followers don't dare be drunk, I think, before their captain."

He exited.

Alone, Sir Petronel said to himself, "I wish I might lead them to no hotter and no more dangerous service, until our Virginian gold were in our purses!"

"Virginia" was the word then used for the North American coast north of Florida. It was not rich in gold, although people believed or hoped it was.

Captain Seagull, Spendall, and Scapethrift were in the Blue Anchor Tavern near Billingsgate, a port. A drawer was also present. Drawers are bartenders.

"Come, drawer, pierce and tap your neatest hogsheads — your best and purest barrels — of wine, and let's have cheer not fit for your Billingsgate tavern but fit for our Virginian colonel," Captain Seagull said. "He will be here quickly."

Hmm. "Cheer not fit for your Billingsgate tavern but fit for our Virginian colonel"? That could be much better cheer — drink — than usual. Or much worse.

"Our Virginian colonel" is Sir Petronel.

"You shall have all things fit, sir," the drawer said. "Would it please you to have any more wine?

"More wine, slave?" Spendall said. "Whether we drink it or instead spill it, the answer is to draw more wine from the tap."

"Fill all the drinking pots in your house with all sorts of liquor," Scapethrift said, "and let them wait on us here like soldiers in their pewter coats of armor. And although we do not employ them now, yet we will maintain them until we do."

Although they would not drink all the pewter pots of wine now, they would keep the pots full until they did drink them.

"Said like an honorable captain," the drawer said. "You shall have all you can command, sir."

"Come, boys, Virginia longs until we share the rest of her maidenhead," Captain Seagull said.

Virginia was still unspoiled country: It metaphorically still had its maidenhood, aka virginity.

Captain Seagull now talked about Virginia. He made it sound like a utopia, but much of what he said was wishful thinking. He either believed what he said, or he was exaggerating to provide entertainment for his audience.

Spendall asked, "Why, is she inhabited already with any English?"

Captain Seagull answered, "A whole country of English is there, man, bred of those who were left there in 1579. They have married with the Indians and make them bring forth as beautiful faces as any we have in England, and therefore the Indians are so in love with them that all the treasure they have, they lay at their feet."

In reality, the first settlers arrived in Virginia in 1585, and they returned to England in 1586. The settlers of 1587 disappeared and became known as the "Lost Colony."

And at first, the Native Americans were friendly, but they turned hostile after bad behavior by the settlers.

"But is there such treasure there, Captain, as I have heard?" Scapethrift asked.

Captain Seagull answered:

"I tell thee, gold is more plentiful there than copper is with us, and for as much red copper as I can bring, I'll have thrice the weight in gold.

"Why, man, all their pans to catch dripping grease from cooking meat and all their chamber pots are pure gold; and all the chains with which they chain up their streets are massive gold chains; all the prisoners they take are fettered in gold."

Some streets could be chained off for traffic control.

Captain Seagull continued:

"And as for rubies and diamonds, they go forth on holidays and gather them by the seashore to hang on their children's coats and stick in their caps, as commonly as our children wear saffron-gilt — imitation gold — brooches and groats with holes in them."

These groats are coins that have holes drilled in them so they can be made into necklaces.

"And is it also a pleasant country?" Scapethrift asked.

Captain Seagull answered:

"As ever the sun shined on; temperate and full of all sorts of excellent viands — all kinds of excellent food. Wild boar is as common there as our tamest bacon is here, venison is as common there as our mutton is here.

"And then you shall live freely there, without sergeants [arresting officers], or courtiers, or lawyers, or intelligencers [informers]; only a few industrious Scots, perhaps, who indeed are dispersed over the face of the whole earth. But as for them, there are no greater friends to Englishmen and England — when they are not in England but are in the world — than they are.

"And for my part, I wish a hundred thousand of them were there in Virginia, for we are all one countrymen now and ruled by one king named James, you know, and we should find ten times more comfort of them there than we do here."

King James I of England was also King James VI of Scotland.

Captain Seagull continued:

"Then for your means to advancement there, it is simple and not preposterously and perversely mixed: You may be an alderman there and never be a scavenger [a street cleaner]; you may be a nobleman and never be a slave. You may come to preferment enough and never be a pander; you may come to riches and fortune enough and have never the more villainy nor the less wit."

"God's me!" Spendall said. "And how far is it thither?"

Captain Seagull said:

"Some six weeks' sail, no more, with any indifferent — moderately — good wind.

"And if I get to any part of the coast of Africa, I'll sail thither with any wind. Or when I come to Cape Finisterre, the westernmost point of Spain, there's a foreright — favorable — wind that will continually waft us until we come to Virginia.

"Look, our colonel's come."

Sir Petronel entered the scene. Following him was the drawer.

Sir Petronel said:

"Well met, good Captain Seagull, and my noble gentlemen!

"Now the sweet hour of our freedom from debt and arrest is at hand. Come, drawer. Fill us some carouses — some full cups of wine — and prepare us for the mirth that will be occasioned soon."

The drawer poured wine and then exited.

Sir Petronel continued:

"Here will soon be a pretty wench, gentlemen, who will bear us company all our voyage."

Captain Seagull said, "Whatsoever she is, here's to her health, noble Colonel, both with cap and knee."

He removed his cap, knelt, and drank.

When the sailors and others drank toasts and healths, they removed their caps and knelt.

Sir Petronel said:

"Thanks, kind Captain Seagull. She's one I love dearly, and her identity must not be known until we are free from all who know us. And so, gentlemen, here's to her health!"

Spendall and Scapethrift said together, "Let it come, worthy Colonel! We do hunger and thirst for it."

They drank to her health and to her freedom.

"Before heaven, you have hit the phrase of one whom her presence will touch from the foot to the forehead, if ye knew it," Sir Petronel said.

"Touch" can mean 1) affect, and 2) injure.

Security's catchphrase was "hunger and thirst for it."

"Why, then, we will join his forehead with her health in our toast, sir," Spendall said. "And Captain Scapethrift, here's to them both."

The woman's husband's forehead would have horns due to his being made a cuckold. The woman, of course, is Winifred, Security's young wife.

All knelt and drank to the mystery woman.

Security and Bramble entered the scene.

Seeing all kneeling, Security said, "Look, look, Master Bramble! Before heaven, their voyage cannot but prosper; they are on their knees for success to it."

He thought that they were praying for a successful voyage, not toasting his prospective cuckolding.

"And they pray to God Bacchus," Bramble said.

Bacchus is the god of wine.

"God save my brave colonel, with all his tall — brave — captains and corporals!" Security said. "See, sir, my worshipful learned counsel, Master Bramble, has come to take his leave of you."

As he and the sailors rose, Sir Petronel said:

"Worshipful Master Bramble, how far do you draw us into the sweet briar of your kindness?"

"Sweet briars" are wild roses, and they are considered to be a type of bramble: a prickly shrub.

Sir Petronel continued:

"Come, Captain Seagull, another health to this rare Bramble, who has never a prick about him."

"Never a prick" can mean 1) never a thorn, aka no prickliness, or 2) never an erection.

"I pledge his most smooth disposition, sir," Captain Seagull said. "Come, Master Security, bend your supporters — your legs — and pledge this notorious — notable — health here."

"Bend your legs likewise, Master Bramble, for it is you who shall pledge me," Security said.

"Not so, Master Security," Captain Seagull said. "He must not pledge his own health."

Bramble would have to wait to pledge Security's health; right now, everyone was pledging Bramble's health.

Security said, "No, Master Captain?"

Quicksilver and Winifred (Security's disguised young wife) entered the scene.

"Why, then, here's one who is fitly come to do him that honor," Security said.

Quicksilver could pledge Bramble's health. He could do that fitly because Winifred was not Bramble's wife.

Quicksilver said to Sir Petronel, "Here's the gentlewoman — your cousin, sir — whom with much entreaty I have brought to take her leave of you in a tavern. Because she is ashamed to be in a tavern, you must pardon her if she does not take off her mask."

Masks were worn for protection from the sun as well as for anonymity.

"Pardon me, sweet cousin," Sir Petronel said. "My kind desire to see you before I went made me so importunate as to entreat your presence here."

"How are you now, Master Francis?" Security asked. "Have you honored this presence with a fair gentlewoman?"

"Please, sir, take no notice of her, for she will not be known to you," Francis "Frank" Quicksilver replied.

If Security were impotent, he could not know her Biblically.

"But my learned counsel, Master Bramble here, I hope may know her," Security said.

"Know her" can mean 1) learn who she is, or 2) have sex with her (that is, Biblically know her).

"No more than you, sir, at this time," Quicksilver said. "His learning must teach him to pardon her."

Security said:

"Well, God pardon her for my part, and I do, I'll be sworn.

"And so, Master Francis, here's to all who are going eastward tonight towards Cuckold's Haven; and so to the health of Master Bramble."

Frank Quicksilver knelt and said:

"I pledge it, sir.

"Has the pledging cup gone round, captains? Has everyone partaken of the health?"

"It has, sweet Frank, and the round closes with thee," Captain Seagull said.

"Well, sir, here's to all eastward and toward — promising — cuckolds," Quicksilver said, "and so to famous Cuckold's Haven so fatally — ominously — remembered."

He drank and then rose to his feet.

Cuckold's Haven was a place on the Surrey shore of the Thames River that was marked by a pair of horns displayed on a tall pole. Supposedly, King John I of England had made a miller a cuckold there.

Sir Petronel said to the disguised Winifred, "Nay, please, coz, don't weep."

"Coz" means 1) relative (not necessarily a cousin), or 2) friend.

He then said, "Gossip Security?"

"Aye, my brave gossip?" Security replied.

"May I have a word with you, please, sir?" Sir Petronel asked.

He then said quietly to Security:

"Our friend, Mistress Bramble here, is so dissolved in tears that she drowns the whole mirth of our meeting.

"Sweet gossip, take her aside and comfort her."

Not recognizing his own disguised wife, Security said quietly to her:

"Pity of all true love, Mistress Bramble.

"What! Do you weep at enjoying your love?

"What's the reason, lady? Is it because your husband is so near, and your heart earns — that is, grieves — to have a little abused and deceived him? Alas, alas, the offence is too common to be respected and taken seriously."

The offense is adultery.

Security continued:

"So great a grace has seldom chanced to so unthankful a woman, to be rid of an old jealous dotard, to enjoy the arms of a loving young knight that, when your prickless Bramble is withered with grief at your loss, will make you flourish afresh in the bed of a lady."

"Prickless" Bramble has a bawdy meaning, but it can also mean "lacks sharp thorns."

"Withered" can mean "unerect."

The drawer entered the scene and said:

"Sir Petronel, here's one of your watermen — hired boatmen — come to tell you it will be flood tide for the next three hours, and that it will be dangerous going against the tide."

It was just before high tide, and the current would be strong.

The drawer continued:

"For the sky is overcast, and there was a porpoise even now seen at London Bridge, which is always the messenger of tempests, he says."

Sir Petronel said:

"A porpoise? What's that to the purpose? Command him, if he love his life, to wait for us. Can't we reach the shipping center of Blackwall, where my ship lies, against the tide and in spite of tempests?

"Captains and gentlemen, we'll begin a new ceremony at the beginning of our voyage, which I believe will be followed by all future adventurers."

"What's that, good Colonel?" Captain Seagull asked.

"This, Captain Seagull," Sir Petronel said. "We'll have our provided supper brought aboard Sir Francis Drake's ship that has compassed the world, where with full cups and banquets — light food and desserts — we will do sacrifice for a prosperous voyage. My mind suggests to me that some good spirits of the waters should haunt her deserted ribs — her unmanned hull — and be auspicious to all who honor her memory, and will with like orgies — that is, ceremonies — begin their voyages."

Sir Francis Drake's ship was named *Golden Hind*. The circumnavigation took place from 1577-1580.

"Rarely conceited — excellently devised!" Captain Seagull said. "One health more to this motion, aka proposal, and let's go aboard to perform it. He who will not this night be drunk, may he never be sober!"

All encircled the disguised Winifred, danced a drunken round, and drank carouses.

A carouse is a big drink of liquor. It is full-out drinking.

Bramble said:

"Sir Petronel and his honorable captains, in these youthful activities, we old servitors may be spared. We came only to take our leaves, and with one health to you all, I'll be bold to do so.

"Here, neighbor Security, to the health of Sir Petronel and all his captains!"

He drank.

Security said:

"You must bend the knee then, Master Bramble."

Bramble and Security knelt.

Security then said:

"So, now I am for you. I have one corner of my brain, I hope, fit to bear one carouse more.

"Here, lady, to you who are encompassed there and are ashamed of our company."

They drank and rose.

Security said:

"Ha, ha, ha! By my truth, my learned counsel Master Bramble, my mind runs so of Cuckold's Haven tonight that my head runs over with admiration and wonder."

Hearing the word "cuckold," Bramble whispered to Security about the disguised Winifred, "But isn't that your wife, neighbor?"

Security whispered back, "No, by my truth, Master Bramble. Ha, ha, ha! A pox on all Cuckold's Havens, I say."

Bramble whispered back, "On my faith, I swear that her garments are exceedingly like your wife's."

Yes, the masked Winifred was wearing her best gown.

Security whispered back:

"*Cucullus non facit monachum*, my learned counsel."

Translated, the Latin proverb stated, "A cowl does not make a monk."

In other words: Appearances can be deceiving.

He continued:

"Not all are cuckolds who seem to be so, and not all who seem not to be cuckolds are so.

"Give me your hand, my learned counsel; you and I will sup somewhere else than at Sir Francis Drake's ship tonight."

He then said to Sir Petronel:

"Adieu, my noble gossip."

"Good fortune, brave captains," Bramble said. "May God send ye fair skies!"

"Farewell, my hearts, farewell!" everyone said.

"Gossip, laugh no more at Cuckold's Haven, gossip," Sir Petronel said.

Security said:

"I have finished. I have finished, sir.

"Will you lead, Master Bramble? Ha, ha, ha!"

Security and Bramble exited.

"Captain Seagull, call for a boat," Sir Petronel said.

Everyone except the drawer called, "A boat! A boat! A boat!"

Everyone except the drawer exited.

Alone, the drawer said to himself, "You're in a proper state, indeed, to take a boat, especially at this time of night, and against tide and tempest. They say yet, 'Drunken men never take harm'; this night will try the truth of that proverb."

He exited.

— 3.4 —

Alone in his home, Security called:

"What, Winnie! Wife, I say! Out of doors at this time?

"Where should I seek the gadfly?

"Billingsgate! Billingsgate! Billingsgate!

"She's gone with the knight: Sir Petronel! She's gone with the knight! Woe be to thee, Billingsgate! A boat! A boat! A boat! A full hundred marks for a boat!"

He exited to go and try to find his wife.

CHAPTER 4

— 4.1 —

Holding a pair of ox horns, Slitgut stood in front of a pole at Cuckold's Haven.

He said to himself:

"All hail, fair haven of married men only! For there are none but married men who are cuckolds.

"As for my part, I presume not to arrive here except in the behalf of my master, a poor butcher of Eastcheap, who sends me to set up, in honor of Saint Luke, these necessary ensigns — these horns — of his homage."

The butchers of Eastcheap were in charge of providing new ox's horns as needed for the pole at Cuckold's Haven. The ox was the emblem of Saint Luke.

He continued:

"And I got up this morning, thus early, to get up to the top of this famous tree — this pole — that is all fruit and no leaves, to advance this crest — emblem — of my master's occupation."

One fruit of adultery is bastards. This kind of fruit is stone-fruit: Stones are testicles.

He then said:

"Up, then!"

He began to climb the pole.

Slitgut then said:

"Heaven and Saint Luke bless me, so that I am not blown into the Thames as I climb, with this furious tempest! By God's light, I think the devil is abroad in the likeness of a storm, to rob me of my horns. Listen at how he roars!

"Lord, what a coil and uproar the Thames keeps! She bears some unjust, dishonest burden, I believe, and so she kicks and curvets and rears up thus to cast it — to vomit it out. Heaven bless all honest passengers, aka travelers, who are upon her back now! For the bit is out of her mouth, I see, and she will run away with them."

He attached the horns to the top of the pole.

Slitgut continued:

"So, so, I think I have made it look the right way; it runs against London Bridge, as it were, even full butt — it directly faces the London Bridge."

The horns directly faced London, where many cuckolds lived.

The image was of a rampaging bull running full-tilt at the London Bridge.

Slitgut continued:

"And now, let me discover from this lofty prospect — this vantage place — what pranks the rude, turbulent Thames plays in her desperate lunacy.

"Oh, me, here's a boat that has been cast away nearby. Alas, alas, see one of her passengers laboring for his life to land at this haven here; pray heaven he may recover — reach — it! His nearest land is even just under me.

"Hold out yet a little, whosoever thou are, I pray, and take a good heart to thee. Be courageous! It is a man; take a man's heart to thee.

"Just a little further; get up on thy legs, man, now it is shallow enough. So, so, so! Alas, he's down again! Hold thy breath, father. It is a man in a nightcap. So!

"Now he's got up again; now he's past the worst. Yet thanks be to heaven, he comes towards me to a considerable extent — and strongly."

Wet, and without his hat, in a nightcap, collar, etc., Security entered the scene. He had fittingly landed at Cuckold's Haven.

Security said to himself:

"Heaven, I ask thee, how have I offended thee? Where am I cast ashore now, so that I may go a righter way home by land?

"Let me see. Oh, I am scarcely able to look about me. Where is there any sea-mark that I am acquainted with? Where is a landmark I can recognize?"

"Look up, father," Slitgut said. "Are you acquainted with this landmark?"

"What!" Security said. "Landed at Cuckold's Haven? Hell and damnation! I will run back and drown myself."

He fell down.

"Poor man, how weak he is!" Slitgut said. "The water has washed away his strength."

Security said to himself:

"Landed at Cuckold's Haven? If it had not been to die twenty times alive, I would never have escaped death."

He believed that he had escaped death by drowning only so that he could die twenty times from the shame of being a cuckold.

Security continued:

"I will never arise anymore; I will grovel here and eat dirt until I am choked; I will make the gentle earth do that which the cruel water has denied me."

"Alas, good father, be not so desperate," Slitgut said. "Rise, man; if you will, I'll come immediately and lead you home."

"Home?" Security said. "Shall I make any know my home who has known me thus abroad? How low shall I crouch away, so that no eye may see me? I will creep on the earth while I live and never look heaven in the face more."

Creeping on the ground, he exited.

Slitgut said:

"What young planet reigns now, I wonder, that old men are so foolish?"

This society believed in astrology: It believed that planets influenced human behavior. In this case, a malign planet was making old men, who should behave wisely, behave foolishly instead.

Slitgut continued:

"What desperate young swaggerer would have been abroad in such a weather as this, upon the water?"

He looked at the Thames again and said:

"Ay me, see another remnant of this unfortunate shipwreck, or some other!"

"Ay me!" is an expression of regret: Alas! Woe is me! Oh! Ah!

Slitgut continued:

"A woman, indeed, a woman! Although she is almost at Saint Katherine's reformatory for fallen women, I discern her to be a woman, for all her body is above the water, and her clothes swim about her most handsomely. Oh, they bear her up most splendidly!"

Her clothing had trapped air, which kept her afloat like Ophelia's clothing did for a while in *Hamlet*.

Slitgut continued:

"Hasn't a woman reason to love the taking up of her clothes all the better while she lives, because of this?"

Her clothes could be taken up for the purpose of love-making.

Slitgut continued:

"Alas, how busy the rude, unkind Thames is about her!

"A curse on that wave. It will drown her, indeed, it will drown her. Cry God mercy — thank God! — she has escaped it! I thank Heaven she has escaped it.

"Oh, how she swims like a mermaid! May some vigilant body — some watchful person — look out and save her. That's well done: Just where the priest fell in, there's someone who is setting down a ladder and is going to take her up."

This place is where the priest fell in, and the woman will turn out to be a fallen woman.

Slitgut continued:

"God's blessing on thy heart, boy. Now take her up in thy arms and to bed with her."

"To bed with her" can mean 1) put her in a bed so she can be warm, or 2) take her to a bed and have sex with her.

Slitgut continued:

"She's up, she's up! She's a beautiful woman, I promise her to be; the billows dare not devour her."

The drawer from the Blue Anchor Tavern, with Winifred, whom he had rescued, entered the scene. Fittingly, Winifred had been rescued near St. Katherine's reformatory for fallen women.

"How are you now, lady?" the drawer asked.

"Much better, my good friend, than I wish," Winifred said. "I fare as one desperate that she may have lost her fame — her reputation — now that my life is preserved."

The drawer said, "Comfort yourself; that power that preserved you from death can likewise defend you from infamy, howsoever you deserve it. Weren't you the one who took boat, late this night, with a knight and other gentlemen at Billingsgate?"

The knight, of course, was Sir Petronel.

"Miserable as I am, I was," Winifred said.

The drawer said:

"I am glad it was my good luck to come down thus far after you, to a house of my friend's here in Saint Katherine's, since I am now happily made a means to your rescue from the ruthless and pitiless tempest. This tempest, when you took boat, was so extreme, and the gentleman who brought you forth so desperate and unsober, that I feared long before this that I should hear of your shipwreck, and therefore (with little other reason) made thus far this way.

"And this I must tell you, since perhaps you may make use of it: There was left behind you at our tavern, brought by a porter hired by the young gentleman who brought you, a gentlewoman's gown, hat, stockings, and shoes, which if they are yours, and you please to shift — change — your clothing, taking a hard bed here in this house of my friend, I will immediately go and fetch those articles of clothing for you."

The young gentleman, of course, was Quicksilver, who realized that Winifred would need her other dress and some personal items and so had ordered them to be sent to the tavern. Later, because Quicksilver was drunk and therefore forgetful, he had left the tavern with Winifred before the items could be delivered.

Winifred replied:

"Thanks, my good friend, for your more than good news.

"The gown, with all things bound with it, are mine; which if you please to fetch as you have promised, I will boldly receive the kind favor you have offered until your return — entreating you, by all the good you have done in preserving me hitherto, to let no one know what favor you do me, or where such a one as I am has been bestowed, lest you incur me much more damage in my reputation than you have done me pleasure in preserving my life."

The drawer said, "Come in, lady, and put yourself in order. Be assured that nothing but your own pleasure shall be used in your discovery: I won't reveal anything that you wish me not to reveal."

"Thank you, good friend," Winifred said. "The time may come I shall requite you."

The drawer and Winifred exited.

Slitgut looked at the Thames River and said:

"See, see, see! I hold — I bet — my life, there's some other taking up — another person landing — at Wapping, now! Someone is being helped to get out of the water! Look — what a crowd of people cluster around the gallows there!"

Pirates, sea-rovers, and criminals were hung at Wapping, located to the east of St. Katherine's reformatory for fallen women.

Slitgut continued:

"In good truth, it is so. Oh, me! A fine young gentleman! What, and taken up at the gallows? Heaven grant he will not be one day taken down there after hanging. On my life, it is ominous.

"Well, he is delivered for the time. I see the people have all left him; yet I will keep my lookout for a while, to see if any more have been shipwrecked."

Quicksilver, bareheaded and without cloak or sword, entered the scene. Fittingly, he had come ashore near a gallows.

He said to himself:

"Accursed am I that ever I was saved or born!

"How fatal — how ominous — is my sad arrival here! As if the stars and Providence spoke to me and said, 'The drift of all unlawful courses, whatever end they dare propose themselves in frame of — in planning — their licentious policies, they are in the firm order of just destiny the ready highways to our ruins.'"

In other words: Providence says that all sinful courses of action will be punished although those who follow such sinful courses of action had something much different and more pleasant intended. Quicksilver's behavior would lead him to the gallows.

Quicksilver continued:

"I don't know what to do; my wicked hopes are, with this tempest, torn up by the roots.

"Oh, which way shall I bend my desperate steps in which unsufferable shame and misery will not attend them? I will walk this bank and see if I can meet the other relics — the other survivors — of our poor shipwrecked crew or hear of them.

"The knight, alas, was so far gone with wine, and the other three, that I refused their boat and took the hapless woman in another boat. The hapless woman cannot but be sunk, whatever fortune has wrought upon the others' desperate lives."

Sir Petronel, Captain Seagull, Spendall, and Scapethrift had gone in one boat, and Quicksilver and Winifred had gone in another.

Quicksilver exited.

Sir Petronel and Captain Seagull entered the scene. They were bareheaded and without cloaks or swords.

"By God's wounds, Captain, I tell thee we are cast up on the coast of France," Sir Petronel said. "By God's foot, I am not drunk still, I hope! Do thou remember where we were last night?"

"No, by my truth, knight, I don't remember," Captain Seagull said. "But I think that we have been a horrible while upon the water, and in the water."

"Ay me, we are undone forever!" Sir Petronel said. "Have thee any money about thee?"

"Not a penny, by heaven," Captain Seagull said.

"Not a penny between us, and cast ashore in France?" Sir Petronel said.

"In faith, I cannot tell that," Captain Seagull said. "Neither my brains nor my eyes are my own yet."

Two gentlemen entered the scene.

Sir Petronel said:

"By God's foot, won't thou believe me? I know that we are in France by the elevation of the pole, and by the altitude and latitude of the climate, aka land."

The elevation of the pole referred to how high the North Star — the Pole Star — was above the horizon, but if one believes that Frenchmen are especially lascivious, it could refer to the elevation of a different kind of "pole."

Sir Petronel said:

"See, here comes a couple of French gentlemen; I knew we were in France. Do thou think our Englishmen are so Frenchified that a man doesn't know whether he is in France or in England when he sees them? What shall we do? We must even go to them and entreat some relief of them. Life is sweet, and we have no other means to relieve our lives now but their charities."

Many men followed French fashions and so were Frenchified: They looked, in some ways, like Frenchmen.

"Please, beg them for help, then," Captain Seagull said. "You can speak French."

Sir Petronel, who could speak rough — ungrammatical — French, said:

"*Monsieur, plaît-il d'avoir pitié de nôtre grand infortunes? Je suis un poure [pauvre? = poor; poivre? or povre? = pepper] chevalier d'Angleterre qui a souffri l'infortune de naufrage.*"

["Sir, would you like to have pity on our great misfortunes? I am a (poor or pepper) knight of England who suffered the misfortune of shipwreck."]

The first gentleman, who could speak French, asked:

"*Un poure chevalier d'Angleterre?*"

Pauvre means "poor." *Poivre* and *povre* mean "pepper."

["A (poor or pepper) knight from England?"]

Possibly, the first gentleman was mocking Sir Petronel's French. But, to be sure, Sir Petronel's life was peppered — seasoned — with poverty.

Sir Petronel said:

"*Oui, monsieur, il est trop vrai; mais vous savez bien, nous sommes touts suject à fortune.*"

["Yes, sir, it is too true; but you know well, we are all subject to fortune."]

"A poor knight of England?" the second gentleman said. "A poor knight of Windsor, aren't you?"

Impoverished military pensioners lived at Windsor.

The second gentleman continued:

"Why do you speak this broken French, when you're a whole Englishman?

"On what coast do you think you are?"

Sir Petronel replied, "On the coast of France, sir."

"On the coast of Dogs, sir," the first gentleman said. "You're on the Isle of Dogs, I tell you."

The Isle of Dogs was a peninsula on the north side of the Thames, and many debtors lived there. It was fitting that Sir Petronel had landed there.

The first gentleman continued:

"I see you've been washed in the Thames here, and I believe you were drowned in a tavern before, or else you would never have taken boat in such a dawning as this was.

"Farewell, farewell, we will not know you and ask your names for shaming of you."

Using a Scottish accent, the first gentleman said to the second gentleman, "I ken the man weel; he's one of those thirty-pound knights."

The second gentleman replied, "No, no, this is he who stole his knighthood on the grand day for four pounds, giving to a page all the money in his purse, I wot [know] well."

The grand day was the day King James VI of Scotland became also King James I of England.

The two gentlemen exited.

"By God's death, Colonel, I knew you were overshot," Captain Seagull said.

Sir Petronel said:

"Sure I think now, indeed, Captain Seagull, we were something overshot."

Sir Petronel had vastly over-estimated how far they had traveled, and they had drunk too much alcohol and were vastly intoxicated.

Quicksilver entered the scene.

Sir Petronel said:

"What! My sweet Frank Quicksilver! Do thou survive to make me rejoice? But what, nobody at thy heels, Frank? Ay me, what has become of poor Mistress Security?"

"Indeed, she has gone quite from her name, as she has from her reputation, I think," Quicksilver said. "I left her to the mercy of the water."

As far as Quicksilver knew, Mrs. Security was far from being secure, and far from having a good reputation.

"Let her go. Let her go," Captain Seagull said. "Let us go to our ship at Blackwall and shift us — let's change out of these wet clothes."

Sir Petronel said:

"Nay, by my troth, let our clothes rot upon us, and let us rot in them.

"Twenty to one our ship has been attached — has been seized — by this time. If we set her not under sail this last tide, I never looked for any other.

"Woe, woe is me, what shall become of us? The last money we could raise, the greedy Thames River has devoured, and if our ship has been attached, there is no hope that can relieve us."

"By God's foot, knight, what an unknightly faintheartedness transports thee and makes thee forget thyself!" Frank Quicksilver said. "Even if our ship would sink, and even if all the world that's beyond us — Virginia — would be taken away from us, I hope I have some tricks in this brain of mine that shall not let us perish."

"Well said, Frank, truly," Captain Seagull said. "Oh, my nimble-spirited Quicksilver, before God I wish that thou had been our colonel!"

The "colonel" — the leader — had been Sir Petronel.

"I like his spirit very much, but I see no means he has to support that spirit," Sir Petronel said.

"Bah, knight, I have more means than thou are aware of," Quicksilver said. "I have not lived among goldsmiths and goldmakers all this while but I have learned something worthy of my time with them. And, not to let thee stink where thou stand, knight, I'll let thee know some of my skill presently."

One way for Sir Petronel to stink where he stands is to beshit himself. One reason for doing that is out of fear, including out of fear of being in a bad and impoverished situation.

"Do, good Frank," Captain Seagull said, "I ask thee to."

"I will blanch and whiten copper so cunningly to make it look so look like silver that it shall pass almost all tests except *the* test," Quicksilver said. "It shall endure malleation, it shall have the ponderosity of Luna, and it shall have the tenacity of Luna and be by no means friable."

In other words, it shall pass almost every test. *The* test would be to melt it so it could be purified; only then would the deception be revealed. Purification means separating silver from base metals such as copper.

The whitened copper (fake silver), however, can pass other tests. It can be beaten and not break, it will weigh as much as Luna (real silver), it will have the strength of Luna (real silver), and it will not crumble and be reduced to powder.

"By God's light, where did thou learn these terms, I wonder?" Sir Petronel said.

"Tush, knight, the terms of this art every ignorant quacksalver is perfect in," Quicksilver said.

Quacksalvers are pretenders to knowledge. For example, some people pretend to have medical knowledge, but don't. These people are known as quacks.

Quicksilver continued:

"But I'll tell you how you yourself shall blanch copper thus cunningly.

"Take arsenic, otherwise called realga [arsenic disulphide], which indeed is plain ratsbane [rat poison]; sublime it three or four times [heat to vaporize and then cool to solidify three or four times]; then take the sublimate of this realga and put it into a glass vessel, into chymia [kemia, aka chemical analysis], and let it have a convenient decoction natural [time to mature over heat], four-and-twenty hours, and the compound will become perfectly fixed [solid]. Then take this fixed powder and project it upon [apply it to] well-purged [well-washed] copper, *et habebis magisterium.*"

"*Et habebis magisterium*" is Latin for "And you will have the philosopher's stone."

The philosopher's stone was supposed to be able to turn base metals into precious metals, such as turning copper into silver. Of course, Quicksilver's chemical process would make copper only look like silver — if it worked.

Alchemists sought the knowledge of how to make the philosopher's stone. Such a stone does not exist, and some con men took advantage of other people's credulity. See Ben Jonson's *The Alchemist*.

"Excellent, Frank, let us hug thee!" Sir Petronel and Captain Seagull said.

Quicksilver said, "Nay, this I will do besides: I'll take you off twelvepence from every angel [a gold coin], with a kind of *aquafortis* [nitric acid], and never deface any part of the image."

This was called "washing" currency: taking away some of the gold without removing the image on the gold coin. Quicksilver was saying that he could extract gold worth one shilling from each ten-shilling coin. Of course, doing this reduces the coin's weight, and doing that was illegal.

"But then it will lack weight," Sir Petronel said.

Quicksilver said:

"You shall restore that thus: take your *sal achyme* [dry salts, aka salt without chyme, aka juice] prepared, and your distilled urine, and let your angels lie in it but four-and-twenty hours, and they shall have their perfect weight again.

"Come on, now, I hope this is enough to put some spirit into your livers and give you courage; I'll infuse more courage into you another time.

"We have saluted and paid our respects to the proud air long enough with our bare sconces — our bare heads. Now I will take you to a wench's house of mine at London, there make shift to shift us, and afterward we will take such fortunes as the stars shall assign us."

The wench was Sindefy; they would change into dry clothes at her house.

"Notable Frank!" Sir Petronel and Captain Seagull said. "We will forever adore thee."

Everyone except Slitgut exited.

The drawer and Winifred, who was wearing clean, dry clothing, entered the scene.

Winifred said:

"Now, sweet friend, you have brought me near enough your tavern, which I desired so that I might with some color — plausible excuse — be seen near, inquiring for my husband; who, I must tell you, stole thither last night with my wet gown we have left at your friend's — which, to continue your former honest kindness, let me ask you to please keep secret from the knowledge of anyone.

"And so, with all vow of your requital, let me now entreat you to leave me to my woman's wit and fortune."

Winifred would use her women's wit to convince her husband that she had been faithful to him and had not been the woman he had seen in the tavern.

"All shall be done that you desire," the drawer said, "and so, I hope that all the fortune you can wish for will attend you!"

The drawer exited.

Security entered the scene, and he said:

"I will once more go to this unhappy tavern before I change one more rag of mine, so that I may there know what is left behind, and what news there is of their passengers.

"I have bought myself a hat and collar with the little money I had about me and made the street passersby a little break from staring at my nightcap."

"Oh, my dear husband!" Winifred said. "Where have you been this last night? All night abroad at taverns? Rob me of my garments? And behave as one run away from me? Alas! Is this seemly and fitting for a man of your credit? Of your age and affection to your wife?"

"What should I say?" Security said. "How miraculously does this turn out? Wasn't I at home and called thee last night?"

"Yes, sir, the harmless, innocent sleep you broke," Winifred said, "and my answer to you would have witnessed it, if you had had the patience to have stayed and answered me. But your so sudden retreat made me imagine you were gone to Master Bramble's, and so I rested patient and hopeful of your coming again until this your surprising and unbelievable absence brought me abroad, with no less than wonder, to seek you where the false knight had carried you."

Of course, the false knight was Sir Petronel.

"Villain and monster that I was, how have I abused thee!" Security said. "I was suddenly gone indeed, for my sudden jealousy transferred me: It carried me away and changed me. I will say no more but this, dear wife: I suspected thee of infidelity."

"Did you suspect me?" Winifred asked. "Did you think that I was unfaithful?"

"Don't talk about it, I beg thee," Security said. "I am ashamed to imagine it. I will go home, I will go home, and every morning on my knees I will ask thee heartily for forgiveness."

Security and Winifred exited.

Alone, Slitgut said to himself:

"Now I will descend my honorable prospect, the farthest seeing sea-mark of the world."

On the ground, he continued:

"No marvel then if I could see two miles about me."

From the top of the pole, he had seen a great distance.

He continued:

"I hope the red — fiery and full-of-lightning — tempest's anger is now blown over, which surely I think that heaven sent as a punishment for profaning holy Saint Luke's memory with so ridiculous a custom.

"Thou dishonest satire, farewell to honest married men; farewell to all sorts and degrees of thee!"

The dishonest satire was a parody of infidelity: the set of ox horns at the top of the pole.

Horns are the sign of cuckolds.

Slitgut said his farewells to various kinds of horns:

"Farewell, thou horn of hunger [dinner horn] that calls the Inns of Court to their manger [dinner table].

"Farewell, thou horn of abundance [cornucopia] that adorns — and adds horns to — the headsmen [head men, and horn-headed men, aka cuckolds] of the commonwealth.

"Farewell, thou horn of direction that is the city lantern."

City lanterns are street lights: lanterns sided with thin, transparent slices of horn.

Slitgut continued with his farewells to various kinds of horns:

"Farewell, thou horn of pleasure, the ensign of the huntsman."

In addition to a hunting horn, a horn of pleasure can be a penis. Huntsmen can hunt game, or they can hunt women.

Slitgut continued:

"Farewell, thou horn of destiny, the ensign of the married man."

In this cynical satire, married men are destined to be cuckolded and so receive the horn of destiny.

Slitgut concluded:

"Farewell, thou horn tree that bears nothing but stone fruit!"

"Stone fruit," of course, is the fruit of stones, aka testicles: bastards.

Alone, Touchstone complained to himself:

"Ha, sirrah! Does my knight adventurer think we can — we know — no point of our compass? Don't we know north-north-east, north-east-and-by-east, east-and-by-north, nor plain eastward? Ha! Have we never heard of Virginia, nor the *Cavallaria*, nor the *Colonoria*?"

Caballaria means a land tenant who is required, in times of war, to provide a soldier on horseback.

The Latin *colonus* means "husbandman," aka "farming tenant."

Sir Petronel of course, was a knight, and someone who hoped to make his fortune in Virginia. One way to do that was to establish a plantation.

Touchstone continued:

"Can we discover no discoveries?

"Well, my errant Sir Flash, and my runagate — my renegade — Quicksilver, you may drink drunk, crack open containers of alcohol and drink the contents, hurl away a brown dozen — a full dozen, of Monmouth sailors' caps or so in sea-ceremony to your *bon voyage* —"

The Earl of Essex once threw his cap in the sea out of an excess of happiness when he learned that the city of Cadiz would be attacked: Ralegh had persuaded Lord Howard of Effingham to undertake the attack.

Touchstone continued:

"— but as for reaching any coast save the coast of Kent or Essex with this tide or with this fleet, I'll be your warrant for a Gravesend toast."

A Gravesend toast is cold toast, and so it is something not worth much.

Touchstone continued:

"There's that gone before which will stay your admiral and vice-admiral and rear-admiral, were they all — as they are — but one pinnace and under sail, as well as a remora, don't doubt it; and from this sconce, without either powder or shot.

"Work upon that now!"

A sconce is 1) a fort, or 2) a head.

The admiral and vice-admiral and rear-admiral are all ships that carry important officers. Sir Petronel's ship is a pinnace: a small ship. The admiral is the flagship.

A remora was a type of fish that was thought to be able to attach itself to a ship and retard its progress.

Touchstone had given the order for Sir Petronel's ship to be seized.

Touchstone continued:

"Nay, if you'll show tricks, we'll vie with you a little."

"To show tricks" is 1) to practice deception, or 2) to show your playing cards.

"To vie" is 1) to contend, or 2) to make a bet.

Touchstone continued:

"My daughter, his lady, was sent eastward, by land, to a castle of his in the air — in what region I don't know — and, as I hear, was glad to take up her lodging in her coach, she and her two waiting-women, her maid and her mother, like three snails in a shell, and the coachman on top on them, I think."

Hmm. "... the coachman on top on them ...." Say no more.

Touchstone continued:

"Since then, they have all found the way back again by Weeping Cross: They have repented their actions.

"But I'll not see them. And for two of them, madam and her malkin, they are likely to bite of the bridle for William, as the poor horses have done all this while that hurried them, or else go graze on the common."

If they bite the bridle, they have no food, and so "to bite of the bridle for William" means "to fare badly."

"For William" may mean "as far as I'm concerned."

The malkin — a woman servant or a sexually immoral woman — is Sindefy.

Touchstone continued:

"So should my Dame Touchstone, too, but she has been my cross and source of torment for these past thirty years, and I'll now keep her to frighten away spirits, truly.

"I wonder why I hear no news of my son Golding. He was sent for to go to the Guildhall early this morning, and I marvel at the matter. If I had not laid up comfort and hope in him, I should grow desperate of all.

"Look, he is coming, just when I was thinking about him."

Golding walked over to him.

Touchstone said:

"How are you now, son? What is the news at the Court of Aldermen?"

"Indeed, sir, an incident somewhat strange, else it has little in it worth the reporting," Golding said.

"What?" Touchstone said. "It is not borrowing of money, then?"

"No, sir," Golding said. "It has pleased the worshipful commoners — members of the Common Council — of the city to make me one in their number at presentation of the inquest —"

He had been elected to the Court of Common Council: a great honor. People would refer to him as "Thy Worship" or "Your Worship" or "Master Golding."

"Presentation of the inquest" means "report to a committee of inquiry."

"Ha!" Touchstone said.

Golding continued, "— and the alderman of the ward wherein I dwell to appoint me his deputy —"

"What!" Touchstone said.

To be an alderman's deputy was a great honor.

Golding continued, "— in which place, I have had an oath ministered to me since I went."

Happy at all this good news concerning Golding, Touchstone said:

"Now my dear and happy son! Let me kiss Thy new Worship, and a little boast my own happiness in thee.

"What a fortune was it, or rather my judgment, indeed, for me first to see that in his disposition, which a whole city so conspires and concurs to second and confirm! To be taken into the livery of his company the first day of his freedom!"

Golding had been made a full, respected member of the Guild — the Goldsmiths' Company — the first day after he had been freed from his apprenticeship. And he had been promoted to some high positions.

Touchstone continued rejoicing:

"Now, not a week married, chosen Commoner and Alderman's Deputy in a day! Note but the reward of a thrifty course. The wonder of his time!"

A Commoner is a member of the Court of Common Council.

Touchstone continued:

"Well, I will honor Master Alderman for this act as becomes me, and I shall think the better of the Court of Common Council's wisdom and worship — worthiness — while I live, for thus meeting, or coming just after me, in the opinion of his desert.

"Go forward, my sufficient and able son, and as this is the first, so esteem it the least step to that high and prime honor that expects and awaits thee."

Possibly, the highest honor that Golding could aspire to would be to become an alderman or even the Mayor of London.

"Sir, as I was not ambitious of this, so I covet no higher place," Golding replied. "It has dignity enough if it will just save me from contempt. And I had rather my bearing in this or any other office should add worth to it, than the place should give the least opinion — the least estimation — to me."

Touchstone said:

"Excellently spoken! This modest answer of thine blushes as if it said, 'I will wear scarlet shortly.'"

Aldermen wore scarlet robes.

Touchstone continued:

"Worshipful son! I cannot contain myself; I must tell thee I hope to see thee one of the monuments of our city."

The monuments of the city are the great citizens of the city: those who have accomplished much in public work and in charity.

Touchstone continued:

"And I hope to see thee reckoned among her worthies to be remembered the same day with the Lady Ramsey and grave Gresham, when the famous fable of Whittington and his puss shall be forgotten, and thou and thy acts become the posies — the legends — on memorial plaques for hospitals; when thy name shall be written upon conduits, and thy deeds played in thy lifetime by the best companies of actors and be called their get-penny: their reliable source of income."

Lady Ramsey, the wife of a Mayor of London, was a benefactress of Christ's Hospital.

Sir Thomas Gresham founded the Royal Exchange, the London mercantile center.

According to legend, Richard "Dick" Whittington became rich when he sold his cat — the best mouser in London — at a high price to the King of

Barbary so it could free his mice- and rat-infested palace from rodents. Dick eventually became Mayor of London. He left his fortune to London for the doing of good works, including building water conduits. Some water conduits in London were named for him.

Touchstone continued:

"This I divine. This I prophesy."

Golding said:

"Sir, don't engage your expectation farther than my abilities will answer. I, who know my own strengths, fear them; and there is so seldom a loss in promising the least, that commonly it brings with it a welcome deceit.

Usually, people are happy to learn that their low opinion of someone has been wrong.

Golding then said:

"I have other news for you, sir."

"None more welcome than I have already heard, I am sure," Touchstone said.

Golding said:

"They have their degree of welcome, I dare affirm.

"The Colonel and all his company, this morning putting forth drunk from Billingsgate, had like to have been cast away on this side Greenwich; and (as I have intelligence, by a false brother — an informer) have come straggling into town like so many masterless men — vagrants without a source of income — in their doublets and hose, without hat, or cloak, or any other —"

They had lost their swords, too.

It was a disgrace for a knight or a gallant to be without a sword.

"A miracle!" Touchstone said. "The justice of heaven! Where are they? Let's go quickly and lay for them. Let's set an ambush for them!"

Golding replied, "I have done that already, sir, both by Constables and other officers, who shall arrest them at their old Blue Anchor Tavern, and with less tumult or suspicion than if yourself were seen in it, under color — the pretext — of a great press that is now taking place, and they shall here be brought before me."

The press is impressment: involuntary draft and enrollment as a soldier or a sailor. Vagrants were often pressed into military service.

Touchstone said:

"Prudent and politic — shrewd — son! Disgrace them all that ever thou can; their ship I have already seized for debt.

"How to my wish it falls out, that thou have the place of a justicer — a judge — upon them! I am partly glad of the injury done to me, in that thou may punish it. Be severe in thy place, like a new officer of the first quarter — the first three months — of service. Do not be diverted from sharply executing justice.

"Have you heard how our lady has come back with her train of attendants from the invisible castle?"

"No," Golding said. "Where is she?"

Touchstone said:

"She is inside, but I have not seen her yet, nor her mother, who now begins to wish her daughter undubbed a knight's lady and unmarried, they say, and that she had walked a foot-pace — slowly and surely, as opposed to a court amble — with her sister.

"Here they come; stand back."

Mistress Touchstone, Gertrude, Mildred, and Sindefy entered the scene.

Touchstone said to her daughter Gertrude, who had married Sir Petronel:

"God save Your Ladyship! God save Your good Ladyship! Your Ladyship is welcome in your return from your enchanted castle; so are your beauteous retinue.

"I hear that your knight errant has travelled on strange adventures. Surely in my mind, Your Ladyship has 'fished fair and caught a frog,' as the saying is."

In other words: Your Ladyship has made a bad marriage.

"Speak to your father, madam, and kneel down," Mrs. Touchstone said.

"Kneel?" Gertrude said. "I hope I am not brought so low yet. Although my knight has run away and has sold my land, I am a lady still."

"Your Ladyship says true, madam," her father, Touchstone, said, "and it is fitter and a greater decorum that I should curtsy to you, who are a knight's wife and a lady, than you be brought on your knees to me, who am a poor cullion — a base fellow — and your father."

Children customarily would kneel before their parents and ask for their parents' blessing.

"Ah!" Gertrude said. "My father knows his duty."

She was OK with her father kneeling to her.

"Oh, child!" Mrs. Touchstone said, shocked.

Touchstone said to Gertrude:

"And therefore I do desire Your Ladyship, my good Lady Flash, in all humility, to depart my obscure cottage and return in quest of your bright and most transparent castle, however presently concealed to mortal eyes."

He then took her by the hand, and still speaking to Gertrude, said:

"And as for one poor woman of your train here, I will take her in order that she shall no longer be a charge to you nor help you to spend and cost your ladyship expenses.

"She shall stay at home with me, and not go abroad, nor put you to the pawning of an odd coach-horse, or three wheels, but take part and share with the Touchstone. If we lack, we will not complain — lament — about it to Your Ladyship.

"And so, good madam, with your demoiselle — your maid — here, please you to let us see your straight — erect, and proud — backs in equipage, aka marching order, and in your fancy dress."

He wanted to see Gertrude and Sindefy depart.

Touchstone finished:

"For truly, here is no roost for such chickens as you are or birds of your feather, if it shall please Your Ladyship."

Gertrude said to her father:

"By the Virgin Mary, fist — fart — on your kindness! I thought as much."

She then said to Sindefy:

"Come away, Sin, we shall as soon get a fart from a dead man as a farthing of courtesy here."

"Oh, good sister!" Mildred said.

Gertrude said to Mildred:

"Sister, sir-reverence?"

"Sir-reverence" means "saving your reverence." It is an apology for vulgar language such as "fart." "Sir-reverence" also meant "excrement."

Gertrude then said to Sindefy:

"Come away, I say. Hunger drops out at his nose."

The proverb referred to poverty. Poor people often cannot afford fuel for a fire, and so their noses drip because they catch colds.

Of course, Touchstone had money, and so Gertrude was calling him stingy.

"Oh, madam, fair words never hurt the tongue," Golding said.

"What do you mean by that?" Gertrude said. "You come out with your gold ends — your bits of wisdom — now!"

Mrs. Touchstone said:

"Stay, lady daughter.

"Good husband —."

Touchstone interrupted:

"Wife, no man loves his fetters, even when they are made of gold. I do not wish to have my head fastened under my child's girdle."

He did not want to be forced to obey her commands.

To have one's head under another person's girdle was proverbial for being inferior to that person.

Touchstone continued:

"As she has brewed, so let her drink, in God's name, and suffer the consequences of her actions. She went witless to her wedding; now she may go wisely a-begging.

"It's but honeymoon yet with Her Ladyship: she has coach-horses, apparel, jewels, yet left; she needs care for no friends nor take knowledge of father, mother, brother, sister, or anybody.

"When those are pawned, or spent, perhaps we shall return into the list of her acquaintance."

Gertrude said:

"I scorn your acquaintance, indeed.

"Come, Sin."

"Oh, madam, why do you provoke your father like this?" Mrs. Touchstone asked.

Gertrude and Sindefy exited.

Touchstone said:

"Nay, nay, even let pride go before. Shame will follow after, I promise you."

He then said to his wife:

"Come, why do thou weep now? Thou are not the first good cow who has had an ill calf, I trust."

A proverb stated, "Many a good cow has an ill calf."

A Constable entered the scene and whispered to Golding.

Touchstone asked:

"What's the news with that fellow?"

"Sir, the knight and your man Quicksilver are outside," Golding said. "Will you have them brought in?"

Touchstone said:

"Oh, by all means. Certainly."

The Constable exited.

Touchstone then said:

"And son, here's a chair; appear terrible to them on the first interview. Let them behold the melancholy — the seriousness — of a magistrate and taste the fury of a citizen in office."

"Why, sir, I can do nothing to them unless you charge them with something," Golding said.

"I will charge them and recharge them, rather than authority should lack foil to set it off," Touchstone said.

"Foil" is a thin piece of metal set under a jewel to show off its radiance.

Touchstone would highlight the crimes of Sir Petronel and Quicksilver so that Golding could show off his power to punish them.

He motioned for Golding to sit.

"No, good sir, I will not," Golding said.

He did not want to sit while Touchstone stood.

"Son, it is your place, by all means," Touchstone said.

"Believe it, I will not sit, sir," Golding said.

Sir Petronel and Quicksilver entered the scene. They were guarded by a Constable and some officers.

"How misfortune pursues us still in our misery!" Sir Petronel said.

"I wish that it had been my fortune to have been trussed up and hanged at Wapping rather than ever to have come here!" Quicksilver said.

"Or my fortune, to have famished in the Island of Dogs!" Sir Petronel said. "That would be better than being here now."

"Must Golding sit upon and judge us?" Quicksilver asked.

Recently, they had been apprentices together.

"You might carry an M under your girdle to Master Deputy's Worship," the Constable said.

The "M" was for "Master."

In other words: You should call Golding "Master Golding" and show him respect because he is the Alderman's Deputy.

"Who are those men, Master Constable?" Golding asked.

"If it shall please Your Worship, they are a couple of masterless men whom I have impressed for the Low Countries, sir," Golding said.

English soldiers had been fighting Spanish soldiers in Holland. English garrisons were there.

"Why don't you carry them to Bridewell, according to your order, so that they may be shipped away?" Golding asked.

Bridewell was a workhouse for the poor, and a place where conscripted soldiers stayed.

"If it shall please Your Worship, one of them says he is a knight, and we thought it good to show him to Your Worship for our discharge," the Constable said.

The Constable did not want to impress a knight into involuntary military service. Impressment was for people of lower status. Possibly, he also wanted a fee for his service.

"Which man is he?" Golding asked.

"This man, sir," the Constable said, indicating Sir Petronel.

"And who's the other man?" Golding asked.

"A knight's fellow, sir, if it shall please you," the Constable said.

"What!" Golding said. "A knight and his fellow thus accoutered and attired? Where are their hats and feathers, their rapiers and their cloaks?"

"Oh, they mock us," Quicksilver said to Sir Petronel.

"Nay, truly, sir, they had shed both their feathers and hats, too, before we saw them," the Constable said. "Here's all their possessions, if it shall please you, that we found. They say that knights are now to be known without feathers, like cockerels — game cocks — are known by their spurs, sir."

Knights customarily wore gilt spurs.

"What are their names, do they say?" Golding asked.

Touchstone said to himself, "Very well, this is. Golding should not take knowledge of them in his position as a magistrate, indeed. It is good that he pretends not to know who they are."

"This is Sir Petronel Flash," the Constable said.

"What!" Touchstone said, pretending to be shocked at hearing the name.

"And this is Francis Quicksilver," the Constable said.

Touchstone said to Sir Petronel:

"Is it possible? I thought Your Worship had been gone for Virginia, sir. You are welcome home, sir. Your Worship has made a quick return, it seems, and no doubt a good voyage. Nay, please be covered, sir. Put on your hat."

He was being sarcastic. Sir Petronel had lost his hat in the Thames River.

Touchstone continued:

"How did your store of sea-biscuits hold out, sir?"

He then looked at Quicksilver and said:

"I thought I had seen this gentleman before.

"Good Master Quicksilver! How a degree to the southward has changed you!"

Virginia is south (and west) of England. ("Virginia" was the word then used for the North American coast north of Florida.) Ships going there from London sailed first southeast to Spain. Also, Quicksilver's fortunes had fallen.

Golding asked Touchstone:

"Do you know them, father?"

Sir Petronel and Quicksilver attempted to speak, but Golding said to them:

"Forbear for a little while your attempts to speak; you shall be heard soon."

Touchstone said:

"Yes, Master Deputy. I had a small venture — a small investment — with them in the voyage, a thing called a son-in-law, or so."

Touchstone then said to the Constable and officers:

"Officers, you may let them stand alone; they will not run away, I'll give my word for them. They are a couple of very 'honest' — cough — gentlemen.

"One of them was my apprentice, Master Quicksilver, here, and when he had two years left to serve as my apprentice, he kept his whore and his hunting nag.

"He would play his hundred pounds at gresco or primero — card games that gamblers play — as familiarly (and all on my purse) as any bright piece of crimson clothing on them all.

"He had his trunks of changeable apparel standing at livery and being kept for him for a fee, with his mare [whore], his chest of perfumed linen, and his bathing-tubs, which when I told him of, why he — he was a gentleman, and I was a poor Cheapside groom, aka servant."

Nobles and court officials wore crimson clothing.

Bathing-tubs were used for treating venereal disease.

Touchstone continued:

"The remedy was, we must part. Since that time, he has had the gift of gathering up some small parcels — sums of money — of mine, to the value of five hundred pounds, dispersed among my customers, to furnish this his Virginian venture."

Quicksilver had collected money that was owed to Touchstone, and he had kept it to finance the planned trip to Virginia. This was a capital offense: Quicksilver could hang for it.

Quicksilver had been lending Touchstone's money to gallants when he was an apprentice, and now he had collected those debts.

Touchstone continued:

"In this Virginia venture, this knight was the chief: Sir Flash.

"He is one who married a daughter of mine, ladyfied and lay her, turned two thousand pounds' worth of good land of hers into cash within the first week, bought her a new gown and a coach, sent her to seek her fortune by land while he himself prepared for his fortune by sea, took in fresh flesh — a new woman — at Billingsgate for his own diet, to serve him the whole voyage — the wife of a certain usurer called Security, who has been the broker for them in all this business.

"Please, Master Deputy, work upon that now!"

Golding said, "If my worshipful father has ended —"

"I have, if it shall please Master Deputy," Touchstone said.

Golding began, "Well then, subject to your correction —"

Touchstone whispered to Golding:

"Now, son, come over them with some fine gird — some fine cutting gibe or remark — such as this, 'Knight, you shall be encountered,' that is, you shall be taken to the Counter."

The Counter was a prison; "to be encountered" meant, in the card game primero, "to draw a winning card."

Touchstone continued whispering:

"Or 'Quicksilver, I will put you in a crucible,' or so."

In some alchemical processes, mercury, aka quicksilver, was placed into crucibles and heated.

Golding said:

"Sir Petronel Flash, I am sorry to see such flashes — such outbursts of bad deeds — as these proceed from a gentleman of your quality and rank. For my own part, I could wish I could say I could not see them; but such is the misery of magistrates and men in place — ministers of state who serve the Crown — that they must not shut our eyes when confronted with offenders and ignore them."

He said to the Constable and officers:

"Take him aside."

He then said to Sir Petronel:

"I will hear what you have to say soon, sir."

"I like this well," Touchstone said to himself. "Yet there's some grace — some virtue — left in the knight; he cries."

Golding said:

"Francis Quicksilver, I wish to God that thou had turned quacksalver rather than run into these dissolute and lewd courses. It is a great pity.

"Thou are a proper, handsome young man, of an honest and clean, fine-featured face, somewhat near a good one — God has done his part in thee; but thou have made too much and been too proud of that face, with the rest of thy body; for maintenance of which in neat, fine, and garish attire, only to be looked upon by some light housewives — hussies, aka harlots — and thou have prodigally consumed much of thy master's estate, and being by him gently admonished, at several times, have shown thyself to be haughty and rebellious in thine answers, thundering out uncivil comparisons — satiric similes — requiting all his kindness with a coarse and harsh behavior, never returning thanks for any one benefit, but receiving all as if they had been debts to thee and not courtesies.

"I must tell thee, Francis, these are manifest signs of an ill nature, and God does often punish such pride and *outrecuidance* — arrogance and overweening conceit — with scorn and infamy, which is the worst of misfortune."

Golding asked Touchstone:

"My worshipful father, what do you please to charge them with?"

He then said:

"From the impress I will free them, Master Constable."

"Then I'll leave Your Worship, sir," the Constable said.

"No, you may stay," Golding said. "There will be other matters against them."

"Sir, I do charge this gallant, Master Quicksilver, on suspicion of felony," Touchstone said, "and the knight as being accessary, in the receipt of my goods."

"Oh, God, sir!" Quicksilver said.

He was afraid of being hanged.

Touchstone said:

"Hold thy peace, impudent varlet, hold thy peace!

"With what forehead or face — what impudence! — do thou offer to chop logic and argue with me, having run such a race of riot — such an extravagant course — as thou have done?

"Doesn't the sight of this worshipful man's fortune and temper confound thee, who was thy younger fellow in household, and now has come to have the place of a judge upon thee? Don't thou observe this?

"Which of all thy gallants and gamesters, thy swearers and thy swaggerers, will come now to moan thy misfortune or pity thy penury? They'll look out at a window as thou ride in triumph to Tyburn and cry, 'Yonder goes honest Frank, mad Quicksilver.'"

"Ride in triumph" meant to ride in the executioner's cart to the gallows at Tyburn. Of course, Touchstone was mocking Frank Quicksilver by referring to the triumphal procession of a Roman general after a great victory.

Touchstone continued:

"'He was a free boon — jolly — companion when he had money,' says one."

"Free" can mean liberal and generous and free-spending.

Touchstone continued:

"'Hang him, fool,' says another, 'He could not keep it when he had it.'

"'A pox on his master the cullion,' says a third. 'He has brought him to this.'

"It is true, however, that their pox of pleasure and their piles of perdition would have been better bestowed upon thee, who have ventured for them — for pleasure and perdition — with the best, and by the clew — the thread — of thy knavery brought thyself weeping to the cart of calamity."

"Pox" is syphilis, and "piles" are hemorrhoids.

"Perdition" means damnation.

In other words: It would have been more appropriate for them to curse you.

"Their pox of pleasure" is a lascivious curse, and "their piles of perdition" is a damnable curse.

Quicksilver pleaded, "Worshipful master —"

Touchstone said:

"Don't attempt to speak, crocodile who sheds false tears. I will not hear a sound come from thee. Thou have learned to whine at the play yonder."

In other words: By watching actors in plays, you have learned how to shed fake tears.

Touchstone then said:

"Master Deputy, please commit them both to safe custody until I am able farther to charge them."

"Oh, me, what an unfortunate thing am I!" Quicksilver said.

Sir Petronel asked Touchstone, "Won't you take security, sir?"

Small-s "security" is bail.

Interpreting "security" as "Security," Touchstone said:

"Yes, by the Virgin Mary, I will, Sir Flash, if I can find him and charge him as deep as the best of you. He has been the plotter of all this; he is your engineer — your plotter and schemer — so I hear."

He then said to Golding:

"Master Deputy, you'll dispose of these?

"In the meantime I'll go to my Lord Mayor and get his warrant to seize that serpent Security into my hands and seal up both house and goods to the King's use, or my satisfaction."

"Officers, take them to the Counter," Golding said.

Quicksilver and Sir Petronel said, "Oh, God!"

They were in serious trouble.

Touchstone said:

"Nay, go on, go on.

"You see the issue of your sloth. From sloth comes pleasure, from pleasure comes riot, from riot comes whoring, from whoring comes spending, from spending comes poverty, from poverty comes theft, from theft comes hanging; and there is my Quicksilver fixed."

"Fixed" is an alchemical term meaning "deprived of fluidity and volatility."

In prison, Quicksilver would lose his freedom. He was in a fix.

They exited.

CHAPTER 5
— 5.1 —

Gertrude and Sindefy talked together on a street in London. Their fine clothing had been pawned to get money for food and shelter.

"Ah, Sin!" Gertrude said. "Have thou ever read in the chronicle of any lady and her waiting-woman driven to that extremity that we are in, Sin?"

Chronicles are history books, such as John Stow's *A Summary of the Chronicles of England* or his *The Annals of England*.

"Not I, truly, madam, and if I had, it would be only cold comfort should come out of books, now," Sindefy answered.

Gertrude said:

"Why, in good faith, Sin, I could dine with a lamentable story now."

She sang:

"*O hone, hone, o no nera*, etc."

The Irish *ochoin* means "oh, alas!"

"O no nera" may mean "oh, non-era."

An *era* can be a beginning of a new period in someone's life and it can be a period in someone's life, and a *non* can be a disapproving person.

Gertrude's life had changed, and she had begun a period in her life in which many people, and especially her father, disapproved of her.

A "non-era" can be a period in someone's life in which that person suffers disapproval.

Gertrude then asked:

"Can thou tell never a lamentable story, Sin?"

Sindefy replied:

"None but my own, madam, which is lamentable enough.

"First to be stolen from my friends and relatives, which were worshipful and of good account and esteem, by an apprentice in the habit — clothing — and disguise of a gentleman, and here brought up to London and promised marriage, and now likely to be forsaken, for he is in possibility to be hanged."

Of course, she was talking about Quicksilver.

Sindefy cried.

Gertrude said:

"Nay, don't weep, good Sin.

"My Petronel is in as good possibility as he."

That possibility was of being hung.

Gertrude continued:

"Thy miseries are nothing to mine, Sin. I was more than promised marriage, Sin: I had it, Sin, and I was made a lady, and by a knight, Sin, who is now as good as no knight, Sin.

"And I was born in London, which is more than brought up, Sin; and I am already forsaken, which is past likelihood and more than mere possibility, Sin.

"And instead of land in the country, all my knight's living — his dwelling — lies in the Counter, Sin. There's his castle now!"

The word "living" also means "landed property."

"Which he cannot be forced out of, madam," Sindefy said.

Gertrude said:

"Yes, if he would live hungry a week or two. 'Hunger,' they say, 'breaks stone walls.'

"But he is even well enough served, Sin, in the Counter, because as soon as ever he had got my hand to the sale of my inheritance, he ran away from me, as if I had been his punk — his prostitute — God bless us.

"Would the Knight of the Sun, or Palmerin of England, have treated their ladies so, Sin, or Sir Lancelot, or Sir Tristram?"

All the names were of knights or princes who were heroes of romances.

"I do not know, madam," Sindefy answered.

Gertrude said:

"Then thou know nothing, Sin. Thou are a fool, Sin. The knighthood nowadays are nothing like the knighthood of old time. Our knights are nothing like the old knights.

"They rode on horseback; ours go on foot.

"They were attended by their squires; ours are attended by their lackeys."

Lackeys are footmen.

Gertrude continued:

"They went buckled in their armor; ours are muffled in their cloaks.

"They traveled wildernesses and deserts; ours scarcely dare to walk the streets because of fear of being arrested for debt.

"They were always impelled to engage their honor; ours are always ready to pawn their clothes.

"They would gallop on at sight of a monster; ours run away at the sight of an arresting sergeant.

"They would help poor ladies; ours make poor ladies."

"Aye, madam, they were knights of the Round Table at Winchester who sought adventures," Sindefy said, "but these are knights of the square table in ordinaries, and they sit and play the gambling game known as hazard."

Ordinaries are eating places.

"True, Sin, let him vanish," Gertrude said. "And tell me, what shall we pawn next?"

"Aye, by the Virgin Mary, madam," Sindefy said, "that is a timely consideration, for our hostess — profane woman! — has sworn by bread and salt that she will not trust us for another meal."

Gertrude said:

"Let it stink in her hand, then; I'll not be beholden — indebted — to her.

"Let me see: My jewels are gone, and my gowns, and my red velvet petticoat that I was married in, and my wedding silk stockings, and all thy best apparel, poor Sin.

"In good faith, rather than thou should pawn a rag more, I'd lay my ladyship in lavender, if I knew where."

Pawned clothing was stored in lavender; Gertrude would pawn her title of Lady, if she knew where she could do that.

"Alas, madam, your ladyship!" Sindefy said.

Gertrude said:

"Aye, why? You do not scorn my ladyship, although it is — as I am — in a waistcoat?"

She had pawned her gown and was wearing a short garment for the upper body. Such dress was a mark of a woman of ill-repute.

Gertrude continued:

"God's my life, you are a peat — a pet, a spoiled girl — indeed!

"Do I offer to mortgage my ladyship for you and for your benefit, and do you turn the lip and the 'Alas' to my ladyship? Do you disparage my title?"

"Turn the lip" means "show contempt."

"No, madam, but I question who — I wonder whether anyone — will lend anything upon it," Sindefy said.

Gertrude said:

"Who will? By the Virgin Mary, enough will, I promise you, if you'll seek them out.

"I'm sure I remember the time when I would have given a thousand pounds, if I had had it, to have been a lady, and I hope I alone was not bred and born with that appetite. Some other gentle-born people of the city have the same longing, I trust.

"And for my part, I would afford them a pennyworth — some — of it; my ladyship is little the worse for the wearing, and yet I would bate — reduce — a good deal of the sum. I would lend it — let me see — for forty pounds in hand, Sin — that would apparel us — and ten pounds a year. That would keep me and you, Sin, with additional income earned from our needles as seamstresses, and we should never need to be beholden to our scurvy parents.

"Good Lord, that there are no fairies nowadays, Sin!"

"Why, madam?" Sindefy asked.

Fairies did good deeds for good housekeepers.

Gertrude said:

"To do miracles and bring ladies money.

"Surely, if we lay in a habitually clean house, they would haunt it, Sin. I'll try. I'll sweep the chamber early this evening, and I'll set a dish of water on the hearth. A fairy may come and bring a pearl or a diamond; we do not know, Sin.

"Or there may be a pot of gold hid in the backside — the back of the house — if we had tools to dig for it.

"Why may not we two rise early in the morning, Sin, before anybody is up, and find a jewel in the streets worth a hundred pounds? May not some great court lady, as she comes away from revels — dances or masques — at midnight, look out of her coach as it is running, and lose such a jewel, and we find it? Huh?"

"They are pretty waking dreams, these," Sindefy said.

They were daydreams.

Gertrude said:

"Or may not some old usurer be drunk overnight, with a bag of money, and leave it behind him on a stall, aka a shop counter? For God's sake, Sin, let's rise tomorrow by break of day and see.

"I say, indeed, that if I had as much money as an alderman, I would scatter some of it in the streets for poor ladies to find when their knights were laid up and imprisoned.

"And now I remember my song of the Golden Shower. Why may not I have such a fortune? I'll sing it, and I'll see what luck I shall have after it."

She sang:

"*Fond [Foolish] fables tell of old,*

"*How Jove in Danaë's lap*

"*Fell in a shower of gold,*

"*By which she caught a clap.*

"*Oh, had it been my hap [fortune],*

"*Howe'er the blow doth threaten,*

"*So well I like the play*

"*That I could wish all day*

"*And night to be so beaten.*"

"Caught a clap" meant to suffer a stroke of bad fortune; in this case, it meant to become pregnant.

The "blow" is a sexual thrust.

The "play" is sex.

An oracle had told Danaë's father, King Acrisius of Argos, that her son would kill him. Therefore, he kept her locked up. Jupiter, the lustful king of the gods, however, came to her in a shower of golden rain. Danaë, made pregnant by Jupiter, gave birth to the Greek hero Perseus. King Acrisius put Danaë and Perseus, her son, into a chest and threw it into the sea. Neptune, god of the sea, provided a calm sea, and the chest washed up on the western coast of Italy, where Danaë founded the city of Ardea. Perseus grew up, learned about the prophecy that he would kill his father, and resolved never to go to Argos. Unfortunately, he competed in athletic games elsewhere, his aged father watched the games, and Perseus accidentally killed him with a discus.

Mrs. Touchstone, Gertrude's mother, entered the scene.

Seeing her, Gertrude said, "Oh, here's my mother! Good luck, I hope."

She asked, "Have you brought any money, mother? Please, mother, give me your blessing."

Gertrude knelt, and Mrs. Touchstone wept.

Gertrude said, "Nay, sweet mother, do not weep."

"God bless you!" Mrs. Touchstone said, weeping. "I wish that I were in my grave!"

Gertrude said:

"Nay, dear mother, can you steal no more money from my father?"

Gertrude rose and said:

"Dry your eyes and comfort me.

"Alas, it is my knight's fault, and not mine, that I am in a waistcoat and attired thus simply."

Mrs. Touchstone said:

"Simply? It is better than thou deserve. Never whimper for the matter.

"Thou should have looked before thou had leaped. Thou were on fire to be a lady, and now your ladyship and you may both blow at the coal and become impassioned, for anything I know.

"Self do, self have.

"'The hasty person never lacks woe,' they say."

A Scottish proverb stated, "Let them that are cold blow at the coal."

Another Scottish proverb stated, "It's a cold coal to blow at."

Gertrude said:

"Nay, then, mother, you should have looked to it. A body would think you were the older. I did but my kind, I did."

In other words: Gertrude wished that her mother had warned her about the dangers of the world. Gertrude believed that she herself had simply acted like what she was: a daughter who wished to marry well.

Gertrude continued:

"He was a knight, and I was fit to be a lady. It is not lack of liking but lack of living — lack of income — that severs us."

Gertrude still loved — or at least still lusted after — Sir Petronel.

Gertrude continued:

"And you talk like yourself and a citiner — a citizen and a citizen's wife — in this, indeed. You show what husband you come on, I am sure — you know who you are married to and what kind of man he is, truly."

"Come on" means 1) come from, and 2) have sex with.

Gertrude continued:

"You smell the Touchstone — he who will do more for his daughter who has married a scurvy gold-end man and his apprentice than he will for his other daughter who has wedded a knight and his customer.

"By this light, I think that he is not my legitimate father."

If she was saying what she really thought, then she also thought that her mother had committed adultery or that her "mother" had just been the midwife at her birth. If the latter, then she — Gertrude — was adopted.

"Oh, good madam, do not take up — don't reprimand — your mother so," Sindefy said.

Mrs. Touchstone said:

"Nay, nay, let her even alone.

"Let Her Ladyship grieve me still with her bitter taunts and terms.

"I have not dole — grief — enough to see her in this miserable case, I, without her velvet gowns, without ribbons, without jewels, without French wires, or cheatbread, or quails, or a little dog, or a gentleman usher, or anything indeed, that's fit for a lady —"

French wires were used as supports for elaborate hairstyles.

Cheatbread is bread, but not bread of the highest quality. Despite being a lady, Gertrude could not afford to buy cheatbread.

Sindefy said to herself, "— except her tongue."

Mrs. Touchstone continued:

"And I am not able to relieve her, neither, being kept so short of money by my husband. Well, God knows my heart. I did little think that she should ever have had need of her sister Golding."

Gertrude said:

"Why, mother, I have not yet need of my sister.

"Alas, good mother, be not intoxicate — overly distressed — for me; I am well enough. I would not change husbands with my sister, I.

"The leg of a lark is better than the body of a kite."

Larks were more highly regarded than kites.

Kites are inferior hawks.

"I know that," Mrs. Touchstone said. "But —"

"What, sweet mother, what?" Gertrude asked.

"It's but ill food when nothing's left but the claw," Mrs. Touchstone said.

"That's true, mother," Gertrude said. "Ay me!"

"Nay, sweet ladybird, don't sigh," Mrs. Touchstone said. "Child, madam! Why do you weep thus? Be of good cheer. I shall die if you cry and mar your complexion thus."

The word "complexion" can mean face paint, aka makeup, but Gertrude is too poor to afford it.

"Ladybird" is a term of endearment.

"Alas, mother, what should I do?" Gertrude asked.

"Go to thy sister's, child," Mrs. Touchstone advised. "She'll be proud Thy Ladyship will come under her roof. She'll persuade thy father to release thy knight and redeem thy gowns and thy coach and thy horses, and set thee up again."

"But will she get him to set my knight up, too?" Gertrude asked.

In other words (possibly): Will Mildred get Touchstone to give Sir Petronel enough money to buy back the land he sold? In any case, Gertrude wanted enough money to set her husband up in life.

"That she will, or anything else thou shall ask her," Mrs. Touchstone replied.

"I will begin to love her, if I thought she would do this," Gertrude said.

Mrs. Touchstone said. "Try her, good chuck, I promise thee that she will."

"Chuck" is a term of endearment, like "ladybird."

Gertrude asked Sindefy, "Do thou think she'll do it?"

"Aye, madam, and be glad you will receive it," Sindefy said.

Mrs. Touchstone said:

"That's a good maiden; she tells you the truth.

"Come, I'll take order — arrange payment — for your debts in the alehouse."

Gertrude said, "Go, Sin, and pray for thy Frank, as I will for my Pet."

They exited.

Touchstone, Golding, and Wolf stood together in front of Touchstone's house. Wolf, who was the jailkeeper of the Counter, was carrying letters. The Counter is a prison.

"I will receive no letters, Master Wolf," Touchstone said. "You shall pardon me."

"Good father, let me entreat you to read the letters," Golding said.

Touchstone replied:

"Son Golding, I will not be tempted. I know my own easy nature, and I don't know what a well-penned subtle letter may work upon it. There may be packing — tricks. Do you see?"

"Packing" is fraudulent dealing.

Touchstone then said to Wolf:

"Return with your packet of letters, sir."

"Believe it, sir, you need fear no packing here," Wolf said. "These are but letters of submission, all."

"Sir, I look for no submission," Touchstone said. "I will bear myself in this like blind justice. Work upon that now. When the Sessions — the court hearings — come, they shall hear from me."

"From whom come your letters, Master Wolf?" Golding asked.

"If it shall please you, sir, one comes from Sir Petronel, another from Francis Quicksilver, and a third from old Security, who is almost mad in prison," Wolf replied. "There are two to Your Worship: one from Master Francis, sir, and another from the knight."

He handed the letters to Golding.

Touchstone said:

"I wonder, Master Wolf, why you should travail thus and work so hard in a business so contrary to kind or the nature of your place."

One kind of "kind" is natural disposition.

Wolf the jailkeeper was a kind person, although judging by his name, one would expect his natural disposition to be cruel and wolvish. One could also expect jailkeepers to be cruel.

Touchstone continued:

"That you, being the keeper of a prison, should labor for the release of your prisoners! Whereas I think it would be far more natural and kindly in you to be ranging about for more prisoners, and not let escape these whom you have already under the tooth — in prison — and in your power. But they say that you wolves, when you have sucked the blood once so that they are dry, you have done and finished with them."

Wolf said:

"Sir, Your Worship may descant — discourse and improvise — as you please on my name, but I say that I was never so mortified with any men's discourse or behavior in prison."

To be "mortified" usually means to be "dead" to the world's pleasures and to be moved to engage in spiritual devotion. Wolf meant, however, that he was not dead to the needs of his prisoners.

Wolf continued:

"Yet I have had all sorts of men in the kingdom under my keys — under lock and key — and men of almost all religions in the land, including Papist [Catholic], Protestant [Anglican], Puritan, Brownist, Anabaptist, Millenary, Family of Love, Jew, Turk, infidel, atheist, good fellow, etc."

Brownists were followers of Robert Browne, who believed that congregations ought to elect their pastors.

Anabaptists believed in adult baptism, and they declined to swear oaths to either civil or ecclesiastical authorities.

Millenarists believed that Christ would reign on Earth for one thousand years.

Dutch mystic Hendrick Niclaes founded the Family of Love, which believed in an inward spiritual transformation that would result in a state of perfection.

Good fellows love alcohol and good times. "Good fellow" was also a slang term for a thief.

"And which of all these, thinks Master Wolf, was the best religion?" Golding asked.

"To tell the truth, Master Deputy, they who pay their fees best," Wolf said. "We never examine their consciences farther."

Prisoners would pay for food, lodging (the prison was divided into sections, some more expensive to stay in than others), and other services.

Golding said:

"I believe you, Master Wolf."

He read the letters and then said:

"In good faith, sir, here's a great deal of humility in these letters."

Wolf said:

"Humility, sir? Aye, if Your Worship were an eyewitness of it, you would say so. The knight will stay in the Knights' Ward, do what we can, sir, and Master Quicksilver would stay in the Hole if we would let him."

The Hole is the common dungeon, and it is the cheapest accommodations in the Counter. The Knights' Ward is the second most expensive, with the Masters' Ward being the most expensive.

Wolf continued:

"I never knew or saw prisoners more penitent or more devout. They will sit up all night singing psalms and edifying the whole prison. Only Security sings a note too high, sometimes, because he lies in the Twopenny Ward, far off, and cannot take his tune — he cannot get the correct pitch. The neighbors cannot rest because of him, and they come every morning to ask what godly prisoners we have."

"Which of them is it who is so devout, the knight or the other?" Touchstone asked.

Wolf said:

"Both, sir, but the young man — Quicksilver — especially. I never heard his like. He has cut his hair, too."

Short hair was a sign of unworldliness. Courtiers and gallants wore their hair long.

Sindefy had not betrayed him to the Philistines as Delilah had treated Samson, and Quicksilver had cut his own hair. Assuming that his repentance was sincere, cutting his long hair was a sign of his newfound spiritual strength.

Wolf continued:

"He is so well given — disposed — and he has such good gifts! He can tell you almost all the stories of *The Book of Martyrs* and speak all *The Sick Man's Salve* without book — that is, from memory.

These were religious books. *The Book of Martyrs* was about Protestant martyrs in the time of Queen Mary, a Catholic Queen of England and Ireland whom her Protestant opponents called "Bloody Mary" because of her religious persecution of their faith.

The Sick Man's Salve by Thomas Becom is about having religious faith during times of illness. It is 545 pages long, and yet Quicksilver seems to have memorized most of the stories in it.

Touchstone said:

"Aye, as if he had had grace.

"He was brought up where it grew, I know. Yes, he grew up in a religious household: mine.

"Go on, Master Wolf."

"And he has converted one Fangs, a sergeant, a fellow who could neither write nor read," Wolf said. "Fangs was called the bandog of the Counter, and Quicksilver has brought him already to pare his nails and say his prayers, and it is hoped that he will sell his place shortly and become an intelligencer: an informer."

A bandog is a dog that is kept chained because it is so fierce.

Sergeants were arresting officers who received fees for making arrests. They could sell their position to another person who would take their place.

Touchstone said:

"No more, I am coming — I am weakening — already. If I should give any farther ear and listen any longer, I would be taken in."

He was beginning to become sympathetic to Quicksilver and Sir Petronel.

Touchstone said:

"Adieu, good Master Wolf."

He then said to Golding, his son-in-law:

"Son, I do feel my own weaknesses; do not importune me. Pity is a rheum — an illness — that I am subject to, but I will resist it."

He then said:

"Master Wolf, fish that is cast in dry pools is cast away. Tell Hypocrisy it will not do; I have touched and tried him too often."

"Hypocrisy" is Touchstone's nickname for Quicksilver. Touchstone is determined not to shed sympathetic tears for him because he had tested Quicksilver's character before — often — and Quicksilver had always disappointed him.

"Touched" and "tried" were also goldsmiths' terms. To "touch" meant to test the quality of a gold alloy by rubbing it on a touchstone and examining its color. To "try" precious metal meant to purify it by melting it and removing impurities.

Touchstone continued:

"I am yet proof — tried and tested and armored against appeals for help — and I will remain so. When the Sessions come, they shall hear from me. In the meantime, to all suits, to all entreaties, to all letters, to all tricks, I will be as deaf as an adder and as blind as a beetle; lay my ear to the ground and lock my eyes in my hand, against all temptations."

He exited.

Golding said:

"You see, Master Wolf, how inexorable he is. There is no hope to recover his good will. Please commend me to my brother knight and to my fellow Francis; present them with this small token of my love."

His "brother knight" was Sir Petronel, his brother-in-law.

He gave Wolf money and then said:

"Tell them I wish I could do them any worthier office, but in this it is desperate — it is hopeless. Yet I will not fail to try the uttermost of my power for them.

"And, sir, as far as I have any credit with you, please let them lack for nothing — although I am not ambitious — not eager — that they should know so much."

"Sir, both your actions and words proclaim you to be a true gentleman," Wolf replied. "They shall know only what is fit, and no more."

Holdfast and Bramble spoke together at the Counter. Holdfast was a prison guard.

"Who do you want to speak with, sir?" Holdfast asked.

"I want to speak with a man named Security who is prisoner here," Bramble said.

Holdfast said:

"You're welcome, sir. Stay there; I'll call him to you."

He called:

"Master Security!"

Security's face appeared at a grating. He was being kept in a dark cell.

"Who calls for me?" Security asked.

"Here's a gentleman who would speak with you," Holdfast said.

"Who is he?" Security asked. "Is he one who grafts my forehead, now I am in prison, and comes to see how the horns shoot up and prosper?"

He was worried that he would be cuckolded while in prison: A cuckold's horns could be grafted onto his forehead the way that a branch from one tree can be grafted onto another tree.

"You must pardon him, sir," Holdfast said to Bramble. "The old man is a little crazed with his imprisonment."

As a usurer, Security had sent many to the Counter, a prison for debtors; now he was in that prison.

Security said:

"What have you to say to me, sir? Look here."

Bramble approached the grate.

Security continued:

"My learned counsel, Master Bramble! I beg your mercy, sir. When did you see my wife?"

Bramble replied, "She is now at my house, sir, and she desired — requested — me that I would come to visit you and inquire of you about your case, so that we might work some means to get you out of prison."

Security said:

"My case, Master Bramble, is stone walls and iron grates."

His "case" was 1) his condition, 2) his container, and 3) his legal case.

Security continued:

"You see it; this is the weakest part of it. And, as for getting me out of prison, there is no means but to hang myself and so to be carried out, to prevent which they have here bound me in intolerable bands and shackles."

"Why, but what is it you are in for, sir?" Bramble asked.

Security said:

"For my sins, for my sins, sir, whereof marriage is the greatest.

"Oh, if I had never married, I would have never known this purgatory, to which hell is a kind of cool bath in respect — in comparison.

"My wife's confederacy, sir, with old Touchstone, that she might keep her jubilee and the feast of her new moon. Do you understand me, sir?"

"Confederacy" means 1) conspiracy, and 2) (sexual) intercourse.

Of course, Touchstone had not had confederacy with Security's wife. Have Quicksilver and Sir Petronel fooled him into believing this? If they have, they are not repentant. Or is Security imagining things in his misery?

A jubilee is a time of celebration and release, and the feast of the new moon is a pagan fertility festival.

Every fifty years the Old Testament Jews freed their slaves in a jubilee. The name comes from the ram's horn that was blown to announce the jubilee.

Originally, the new moon was the first crescent moon of the lunar cycle. A crescent moon has horns.

Of course, horns are the sign of the cuckold.

Quicksilver entered the scene and said to Bramble:

"Good sir, go in and talk with him. The light does him harm, and his example will be hurtful to the weak prisoners."

Security was being kept in a dark cell, and the light did hurt his eyes.

Some prisoners are literally weak, and they will be discouraged if Security talks about injured eyes.

Quicksilver then said:

"Bah, father Security, that you'll be still so profane! Will nothing humble you?"

All exited, but as they exited, two prisoners entered the scene, accompanied by a friend.

The friend asked about Quicksilver, "Who's he?"

"Oh, he is a rare — a splendid — young man," the first prisoner said. "Don't you know him?"

"No, I don't," the friend said. "I never saw him that I can remember."

"Why, it is he who was the gallant apprentice of London, Master Touchstone's man — he was his apprentice," the second prisoner, whose name was Toby, said.

"Who, Quicksilver?" the friend asked.

"Aye, this is he," the first prisoner said.

"Is this he?" the friend said. "They say he has been a gallant indeed."

The second prisoner said:

"Oh, he was the royallest — most royal — fellow who ever was bred up in the city!

"He would play his thousand pounds a night at dice, keep knights and lords company, go with them to bawdy-houses; have his six men in a livery, keep a stable of hunting horses, and keep his wench in her velvet gown and her cloth of silver."

Cloth of silver was interwoven with threads of silver, or it was gilded.

Quicksilver was prodigal, but these exploits seem to have come into existence because of rumor.

The second prisoner continued:

"Here's one knight with him here in prison."

"And how miserably he has changed!" the friend said.

"Oh, that's voluntary in him," the first prisoner said. "He gave away all his rich clothes as soon as ever he came in here, among the prisoners, and he will eat food out of the basket for humility."

The basket was an alms basket of food scraps; these scraps were NOT good eating.

"Why will he do so?" the friend asked.

"Alas, he has no hope of life," the second prisoner said. "He mortifies himself. He does but linger on until the Sessions."

According to the second prisoner, Quicksilver expected to be hanged. He was preparing for the next life.

The first prisoner said:

"Oh, he has penned the best thing, which he calls his 'Repentance' or his 'Last Farewell,' that ever you heard. He is a pretty poet, and for prose — you would wonder at and be surprised by how many prisoners he has helped out, with penning petitions for them, and not take a penny."

The petitions were requests for forgiveness of debt or for other forms of charity.

The first prisoner continued:

"Look, this is the knight, in the rug gown."

"Rug" is a coarse fabric. Sir Petronel was wearing a rug gown as a sign of repentance. This was similar to the wearing of sackcloth.

The first prisoner then said:

"Let's stand to the side."

They stood aside and watched the scene.

Sir Petronel, Bramble, and Quicksilver entered the scene.

Bramble said:

"Sir, as for Security's case, I have told him.

"Let's say that he would be condemned to be carted and whipped for a bawd, or so —"

Security had housed Sindefy, Quicksilver's punk.

Bramble continued:

"— why, I'll lay an execution on him of two hundred pounds; let him acknowledge a judgment — he shall do it in half an hour — they shall not all fetch him out without paying the execution, on my word."

This was a legal trick. If Security agreed to pay money — two hundred pounds — to Touchstone, he could not be taken out of prison and carted and whipped until the money was repaid. The authorities would be unwilling to pay that debt, and so Security would not be whipped.

Possibly.

Bramble's legal maneuvers are so twisty and convoluted that understanding them can be difficult — which is probably the point.

"But can't we be bailed out, Master Bramble?" Sir Petronel asked.

Bramble answered:

"Hardly. None of the judges is in town, else you should remove yourself, in spite of Touchstone, with a *habeas corpus*."

Habeas corpus is the legal right to have a court hearing. People cannot be locked up legally for very long unless they have a court hearing first. The court hearing could be about reducing the amount of bail needed to be released from prison.

Bramble continued:

"But if you have a friend to deliver your tale sensibly — that is, appealingly — to some justice of the town, so that he may have feeling of it, do you see, you may be bailed."

One way for the authorities to have the feeling that these men should be released from prison would be to put money into the justice's hand so the justice could feel it.

Another kind of feeling is the feeling of sympathy, but sometimes a bribe is more effective.

Bramble continued:

"For as I understand the case, it is done only *in terrorem* — done only to terrify others as a deterrent to crime — and you shall have a legal action of false imprisonment against him when you come out, and perhaps a thousand pounds costs."

Master Wolf entered the scene.

Seeing him, Quicksilver asked, "How are you now, Master Wolf? What is the news? What return — what answer — do they make?"

Wolf answered, "Indeed, all the news is bad. Yonder will be no letters received. Touchstone says the Sessions shall determine it. Master Deputy Golding, however, commends himself to you, and with this token wishes he could do you other good."

He gave Quicksilver Golding's money.

Quicksilver said:

"I thank him.

"Good Master Bramble, trouble our quiet no more; do not molest us in prison thus with your winding — tricky, devious, and wily — devices and plots. Please depart."

Bramble exited.

Quicksilver continued:

"For my part, I commit my cause to Him Who can succor me; let God work His will.

"Master Wolf, please let this money be distributed among the prisoners and desire — request — them to pray for us."

He returned the money.

"It shall be done, Master Francis," Wolf said.

Francis Quicksilver exited.

"An excellent temperament and disposition!" the first prisoner said.

"Now God send him good luck!" the second prisoner said.

The two prisoners and their friend exited.

"But what did my father-in-law say, Master Wolf?" Sir Petronel asked.

Holdfast entered the scene.

"There is a man who would speak with you, sir," Holdfast said to Wolf.

"I'll tell you soon, Sir Petronel," Wolf said.

Sir Petronel exited.

Wolf asked Holdfast, "Who is it?"

"A gentleman, sir, who will not be seen," Holdfast said.

Golding entered the scene.

Wolf asked:

"Where is he?"

Seeing Golding, he said:

"Master Deputy! Your Worship is welcome —"

"Peace!" Golding said. "Quiet!"

He wanted secrecy.

Wolf said to Holdfast, "Away, sirrah!"

Holdfast exited.

Golding said:

"In good faith, Master Wolf, the estate — the situation and condition — of these gentlemen, for whom you were so recently and willingly a suitor, does much affect me.

"And because I am desirous to do them some fair service, and I find that there is no means to make my father relent so likely as to bring him here to be a spectator of their miseries, I have ventured on a trick, which is to make myself your prisoner, entreating you to immediately go and report it to my father, and, feigning an action at the suit of some third person, request of him by this token" — he gave Wolf a ring — "that he will immediately and with all secrecy come here to be my bail."

As part of the trick, Wolf would say that Golding was in prison because he owed money to someone.

Golding continued:

"This train, aka stratagem, if any, I know will bring him out of his house, and then having him here, I don't doubt but we shall be all fortunate in the eventual outcome."

If Touchstone were to actually see the prisoners, he would feel sympathy for them and he would relieve their distress.

"Sir, I will put on my best speed to effect it," Wolf said. "Please come in."

"Yes, and let me rest and remain concealed, please," Golding said.

He exited.

"See here a benefit truly done, when it is done timely, freely, and to no ambition and ostentation," Wolf said.

He exited.

Touchstone, Mrs. Touchstone, their daughters (Mildred and Gertrude), Sindefy, and Winifred talked together at Touchstone's house.

"I will sail by you and not hear you, like the wise Ulysses," Touchstone said.

Touchstone had gotten the myth wrong. Actually, Ulysses wished to sail by the Sirens and hear them and survive. Other sailors on other ships who had heard the Sirens had jumped overboard and been killed. Therefore, Ulysses ordered his men to stop their ears with beeswax and tie him to the mast and sail by the Sirens. Being tied to the mast kept Ulysses from jumping overboard, and he survived hearing the song of the Sirens.

Mildred knelt and said, "Dear father!"

Mrs. Touchstone knelt and said, "Husband!"

Gertrude knelt and said, "Father!"

Winifred and Sindefy knelt and said, "Master Touchstone!"

"Away, Sirens!" Touchstone said. "I will immure myself against your cries and lock myself up to your lamentations."

"Gentle husband, hear me," Mrs. Touchstone said.

"Father, it is I, father, my Lady Flash," Gertrude said. "My sister and I are friends."

"Good father!" Mildred said.

"Be not hardened, good Master Touchstone," Winifred said.

"Please, sir, be merciful," Sindefy said.

Touchstone said:

"I am deaf, I do not hear you; I have stopped my ears with shoemaker's wax and drunk Lethe and mandragora to forget you."

The water of the Lethe River causes forgetfulness in souls.

The mandragora plant is mandrake, and it has narcotic qualities. It puts people into a deep sleep.

Touchstone continued:

"All that you speak to me I commit to the air."

He exited, and the women rose.

Wolf entered the scene.

"How are things now, Master Wolf?" Mildred asked.

"Where's Master Touchstone?" Wolf said. "I must speak with him immediately. I have lost my breath because of haste."

"What's the matter, sir?" Mildred said. "I pray that all is well!"

"Master Deputy Golding has been arrested upon a writ of execution and desires Touchstone immediately to come to him without delay," Wolf said.

"Ay me!" Mildred said.

She called, "Do you hear me, father?"

From inside, Touchstone said, "Tricks, tricks, confederacy, tricks! I have them in my nose, I scent them."

According to Touchstone, he scented tricks the way that an animal of prey scented hunters.

"Who's that?" Wolf asked. "Master Touchstone?"

"Why, it is Master Wolf himself, husband," Mrs. Touchstone called to her husband.

"Father!" Mildred called.

From an inside room, Touchstone said, "I am deaf still, I say. I will neither yield to the song of the Siren nor the voice of the hyena, the tears of the crocodile nor the howling of the wolf. Avoid my habitation, monsters! Leave!"

People in this society believed that hyenas could imitate the voices of men and lure them to their death.

Wolf called, "Why, you aren't mad, are you, sir? I ask you to look forth and see the token I have brought you, sir."

Touchstone entered the scene and said, "Huh! What token is it?"

Wolf showed him Golding's ring and asked, "Do you know it, sir?"

"My son Golding's ring!" Touchstone said. "Are you in earnest, Master Wolf?"

"Aye, by my faith, sir," Wolf said. "He is in prison and requested me to use all speed and secrecy to you."

Touchstone said:

"Give me my cloak there!"

He then said to the women:

"Please be patient; I am plagued for my austerity."

He said again:

"My cloak!"

He then asked:

"At whose suit, Master Wolf?"

"I'll tell you as we go, sir," Wolf said.

They exited.

141

The two prisoners and their friend talked together in the Counter.

"Why, but is his offence — Quicksilver's crime — such as that he cannot have hope of life — have hope to continue living?" the friend asked.

"Indeed, it would seem so," the first prisoner said, "and it is a great pity, for he is exceedingly penitent."

"They say he is charged only on suspicion of felony yet," the friend said.

"Aye, but his master is a shrewish — that is, ill-natured — fellow," the second prisoner said. "He'll prove great matter against him."

"More than anything else, I'd like to see his 'Farewell,'" the friend said.

Touchstone had written a song of repentance. He believed that he would be sentenced to death, and he planned to sing his "Farewell" as he was carted to the place where he expected to be hung.

"Oh, it is rarely — splendidly — written!" the first prisoner said. "Why, Toby may get him to sing it to you. Quicksilver is not standoffish with anybody."

Toby was the second prisoner's name.

"Oh, he is definitely not standoffish," the second prisoner said. "He wishes that all the world should learn about his repentance, and he thinks he acquires merit in it the more shame he suffers."

In other words: The more shame he feels, the more sincere is his repentance; if he felt no shame, he would not have sincerely repented.

The first prisoner said to the second prisoner, "Please, try and see what thou can do."

"I promise you that he will not deny it, if he is not hoarse with the often repeating of it," the second prisoner said.

He exited.

The first prisoner said, "You never saw a more courteous creature than he is, and the knight, too. The poorest prisoner of the house may command them: They may request favors from them. You shall hear a thing admirably penned."

"Is the knight any scholar, too?" the friend asked. "Is he an author?"

The first prisoner said, "No, but he will speak very well, and discourse admirably of racing horses, and Whitefriars, and against bawds, and of cocks, and he will talk as loud as a hunter, but he is none."

"He is none" can mean 1) he is a not a hunter, and/or 2) he is not a scholar and author.

Whitefriars was a sanctuary for debtors and a haunt of prostitutes.

Wolf and Touchstone entered the scene.

"Please stay here, sir," Wolf said to Touchstone. "I'll call His Worship down to you."

His Worship was Golding.

Wolf exited.

Touchstone stood aside.

Quicksilver and Sir Petronel, who were escorted by the second prisoner, entered the scene.

From another direction, Wolf and Golding entered the scene and stood apart from the others to witness the scene.

The first prisoner said, "See, he has brought him, and the knight, too. Greet him, please."

He then said to Quicksilver, "Sir, this gentleman, upon our report, is very desirous to hear some piece of your 'Repentance.'"

"Sir, with all my heart, and as I told Master Toby, I shall be glad to have any man be a witness of it," Quicksilver said. "And the more openly I profess it, I hope it will appear the heartier and the more unfeigned."

"Who is this?" Touchstone said to himself. "My former serving-man Francis? And my son-in-law?"

"Sir, it is all the testimony I shall leave behind me to the world and my master whom I have so offended," Francis Quicksilver said.

"Good sir!" the friend said.

"I wrote it when my spirits were oppressed," Quicksilver said.

"Aye, I'll be sworn for you, Francis," Sir Petronel said. "What you said is true."

"It is in imitation of Mannington's, he who was hanged at Cambridge, who cut off the horse's head at a blow," Quicksilver said.

George Mannynton [Mannington] wrote "A Woeful Ballad" (1576) an hour before he was executed. It began, "I wail in woe, I plunge in pain."

"So, sir," the friend said.

Quicksilver said, "It is to the tune of 'I wail in woe, I plunge in pain.'"

"An excellent ditty it is, and worthy of a new tune," Sir Petronel said.

Quicksilver sang:

"In Cheapside famous for gold and plate,

"Quicksilver, I did dwell of late.

"I had a master good and kind,

"That would have wrought [fashioned] me to his mind.

"He bade me still [continually], 'Work upon that,'

"But alas, I wrought I knew not what.

"He was a touchstone black but true

"And told me still [continually] what would ensue.

"Yet, woe is me, I would not learn;

"I saw, alas, but could not discern."

The touchstones used to test the purity of gold alloys were often black.

"Excellent!" the friend said. "Excellent well."

Wolf started to move towards Touchstone, but Golding stopped him and said, "Oh, let Quicksilver alone! Touchstone is taken — is captivated — already."

Quicksilver continued singing his song:

"I cast my coat and cap away;

"I went in silks and satins gay.

"False metal of good manners I

"Did daily coin unlawfully.

"I scorned my master, being drunk;

"I kept my gelding and my punk.

"And with a knight, Sir Flash by name,

"Who now is sorry for the same —"

"False metal of good manners" is fake gallantry.

"I thank you, Francis," Sir Petronel said.

Quicksilver continued singing his song:

"I thought by sea to run away,

"But Thames and tempest did me stay."

Touchstone said to himself, "This cannot be feigned, surely. Heaven pardon my severity! The ragged colt may prove to be a good horse."

Golding whispered to Wolf, "How he listens and is transported: He is enraptured by it! He has forgotten me."

Quicksilver continued singing his song:

"Still 'Eastward ho!' was all my word,

"But westward I had no regard.

"Nor never thought what would come after,

"As did, alas, his youngest daughter."

Mildred was the prudent younger daughter. She could consider the results of her own actions and the results of other people's actions.

Westward is the direction toward the Tyburn gallows, and eastward may be the direction of good fortune because it is the opposite direction. But eastward is the direction toward Cuckold's Haven.

Quicksilver and Sir Petronel had wanted to go westward to Virginia, but now it looked as if one or both of them would go westward to Tyburn. Just as on the night of the storm, they had fallen short in their journey.

The word "daughter," then pronounced "dafter," rhymed with "after."

Quicksilver continued:

"At last the black ox trod o'my foot,

"And I saw then what 'longed unto't [belonged to it]."

A black ox is a symbol of ill fortune.

Quicksilver continued:

"Now cry I, 'Touchstone, touch me still,

"'And make me current by thy skill.'"

In other words, the last two lines say:

"Now I cry, 'Touchstone, continue to test me,

"'And make me good metal — and with good mettle — with your skill.'"

Starting to come forward, Touchstone said, "And I will do it, Francis."

Wolf said quietly to Golding, "Stay him, Master Deputy; now is the time; we shall lose the song else."

He wanted Golding to stop Touchstone from approaching Quicksilver now; he wanted to hear the rest of Quicksilver's song.

Golding and Wolf approached Touchstone.

The friend said to Quicksilver, "I say that it is the best song that I ever heard."

"How do you like it, gentlemen?" Quicksilver asked.

"Oh, it is admirable, sir!" the friend and the two prisoners said.

"This stanza now following alludes to the story of Mannington, from whence I took my objective for my invention," Quicksilver said.

He was emulating Mannington, who had written his own song of repentance.

"Please go on, sir," the friend said.

Quicksilver continued singing his song:

"'*O Mannington, thy stories show*

"*Thou cutt'st a horsehead off at a blow,*

"*But I confess, I have not the force*

"*For to cut off the head of a horse.*

"*Yet I desire this grace to win:*

"*That I may cut off the horsehead of Sin*

"*And leave his body in the dust*

"*Of sin's highway and bogs of lust.*

"*Whereby I may take Virtue's purse*

"*And live with her, for better, for worse.*"

Mannington was said to be able to cut off a horse's head with a single blow.

Quicksilver sang that he would like to cut off the horsehead of Sin so that he could take the purse (bag for money) of Virtue and live with her. Of course, this sounds as if he is robbing Virtue.

"Admirable, sir, and excellently conceited — excellently imagined," the friend said.

"Alas, sir," Quicksilver said.

Touchstone said quietly:

"Son Golding and Master Wolf, I thank you. The deceit is welcome —"

The deceit was the pretense that Golding had been arrested and put in the prison.

Touchstone turned to Golding and continued:

"— especially from thee, whose charitable soul in this has shown a high point of wisdom and honesty.

"Listen! I am ravished with his 'Repentance,' and I could stand here a whole apprenticeship to hear him."

The length of a whole apprenticeship was usually seven years.

"Forth, good sir," the friend said to Quicksilver. "Continue."

Quicksilver said, "This is the last part, and the 'Farewell.'"

Quicksilver finished singing his song:

"*Farewell, Cheapside, farewell, sweet trade*

"*Of goldsmiths all that never shall fade.*

"*Farewell, dear fellow prentices [apprentices] all,*

"*And be you warnèd by my fall.*

"*Shun usurers, bawds, and dice and drabs [whores];*

"*Avoid them as you would French scabs [syphilitic sores and scars].*

"*Seek not to go beyond your tether,*

"*But cut your thongs unto your leather.*

"*So shall you thrive by little and little;*

"*Scape [Escape] Tyburn, Counters, and the Spittle.*"

The expression "to cut thongs of others' leather" means "to take what is not rightfully yours."

The full proverb is "It is not honest to make large thongs [out] of others' leather," and it means, "Don't be prodigal at other people's expense."

The variation "cut your thongs unto your leather" means "to live within your means."

Thongs are narrow strips of leather.

The Spittle is the Spital, a hospital for indigent patients. Venereal and other diseases were treated there.

Touchstone came forward and said, "And escape them shall thou, my penitent and dear Francis!"

"Master!" Quicksilver said.

He knelt.

Sir Petronel said, "Father!"

He knelt.

Touchstone said:

"I can no longer forbear to do your humility right. Arise, and let me honor your 'Repentance' with the hearty and joyful embraces of a father and friend's love.

"Quicksilver, thou have eaten into my breast, Quicksilver, with the drops of thy sorrow, and killed the desperate — the despairing — opinion I had of thy reclaim."

The "drops of thy sorrow" are tears.

The inorganic salts of quicksilver, aka mercury, can be corrosive to the skin. Mercury can also dissolve gold.

By "eaten into my breast," Touchstone meant "touched my heart."

Quicksilver's humility had changed Touchstone's former opinion that Quicksilver could not be reclaimed.

Rising, Quicksilver said, "Oh, sir, I am not worthy to see your worshipful face."

Rising, Sir Petronel said, "Forgive me, father."

Touchstone said:

"Speak no more; all former passages — all former events — are forgotten, and here my word shall release you.

"Francis, thank this worthy brother and kind friend."

He wanted Francis Quicksilver to thank Golding and Wolf.

Touchstone then said:

"Master Wolf, I am their bail."

Security shouted in the prison as he ran toward the grate.

Appearing at the grate, he shouted, "Master Touchstone! Master Touchstone!"

"Who's that?" Touchstone asked.

"Security, sir," Wolf said.

"Please, sir, if you'll be won with a song, hear my lamentable tune, too," Security said.

He sang:

"*O Master Touchstone,*

"*My heart is full of woe;*

"*Alas, I am a cuckold,*

"*And why should it be so?*

"*Because I was a usurer*

"*And bawd, as all you know,*

"*For which, again I tell you,*

"*My heart is full of woe.*"

Touchstone said:

"Bring him forth, Master Wolf, and release his restraints."

Wolf exited.

He then returned with Security.

Touchstone said:

"This day shall be sacred to mercy and the mirth of this encounter in the Counter."

Seeing some people coming, he said:

"Look, we are encountered with more suitors."

Suitors are suppliants: They need or want something.

Mrs. Touchstone, Gertrude, Mildred, Sindefy, and Winifred entered the scene.

Touchstone then said:

"Save your breath, save your breath! All things have happened according to your wishes, and we are heartily satisfied in their outcomes."

Gertrude said to Sir Petronel, "Ah, runaway, runaway, have I caught you? And how has my poor knight done all this while?"

"Dear lady-wife, forgive me!" Sir Petronel said.

Gertrude replied:

"As heartily as I would be forgiven, knight."

She knelt and said to Touchstone:

"Dear father, give me your blessing and forgive me, too.

"I have been proud and lascivious, father, and a fool, father; and being raised to the state of a wanton coy thing called a lady, father, I have scorned you, father, and my sister, and my sister's velvet cap, too; and I would make a mouth — an expression of contempt — at the city as I rode through it, and I would stop my ears at Bow-bell."

Bow-bell is the bell at St. Mary-le-bow.

Gertrude continued:

"I have said your beard was a base one, father; and that you looked like Twierpipe, the taborer; and that my mother was only my midwife."

A tabor is a small drum. Often, a taborer would play the tabor with one hand and a pipe — a wind instrument — with the other.

"Now God forgive you, child madam!" Mrs. Touchstone said.

Touchstone said:

"No more repetitions and recitations of past sins."

Gertrude rose.

Touchstone then asked:

"What else is needed to make our harmony full?"

"Only this, sir," Golding said, "that my fellow Francis make amends to Mistress Sindefy with marriage."

"With all my heart," Francis Quicksilver said.

"And Security give her a dower, which shall be all the restitution he shall make of that huge mass he has so unlawfully gotten," Golding said.

"Excellently devised!" Touchstone said. "A good suggestion. What does Master Security say?"

"I say anything, sir," Security said. "I say what you'll have me say. I wish I were no cuckold!"

"Cuckold, husband?" Winifred said. "Why, I think this wearing of yellow has infected you."

"Yellow" is the color of jealousy. Security was wearing yellow.

Touchstone said:

"Why, Master Security, that should be a comfort to you rather than a corrosive to your mental health.

"If you should be a cuckold, it's an argument you have a beautiful woman for your wife.

"Then you shall be much made of; you shall have a store of friends; you shall never lack money; you shall be eased of much of your wedlock 'pain' because others will take it on for you."

In other words: Others will do for you your husbandly duty to your wife in bed.

Touchstone continued:

"Besides, you are a usurer and likely to go to hell, but the devils will never torment you; they'll take you for one of their own race because of your cuckold's horns.

"Again, if you should be a cuckold and don't know it, you are an innocent, and if you know it and endure it, you are a true martyr."

Innocents are 1) guiltless people, or 2) fools.

Martyrs undergo great suffering, and sometimes they die.

Security said:

"I am resolved, sir."

He was resolved to make the best of the situation.

He then said:

"Come hither, Winnie."

He put his arm around her.

Touchstone said:

"Well, then, all are pleased, or shall be soon.

"Master Wolf, you look hungry, I think. Do you have any apparel to lend Francis to change into?"

Francis Quicksilver said, "No, sir, nor do I desire any, but here I make it my suit that I may go home through the streets in these clothes, as a spectacle for people to stare at, or rather an example, to the children of Cheapside."

His suit was 1) his petition to Touchstone, and 2) his prison uniform.

He wanted to wear the prison uniform as he walked through the streets to Touchstone's home.

Touchstone said:

"Thou have thy wish."

He then said to the audience, including the readers of this book:

"Now, London, look about, and in this moral see thy glass [hourglass, aka time] run out.

"Behold the careful father, thrifty son;

"The solemn deeds, which each of us have done;

"The usurer punished, and from fall so steep

"The prodigal child reclaimed, and the lost sheep."

He started to exit, but —

EPILOGUE

— Quicksilver said to Touchstone:

"Stay, sir, I perceive that the multitude are gathered together to view our coming out at the Counter."

He gestured at the audience members in the theatre and said:

"See whether the streets [the pit] and the fronts of the houses [the galleries] are full of people and the windows are filled with ladies as on the solemn day of the pageant!"

The pageant was an annual entertainment to celebrate the investiture of the Lord Mayor of London.

Quicksilver then said to the audience:

"Oh, may you find in this our pageant here

"The same contentment which you came to seek;

"And as that show but draws you once a year,

"May this attract you, hither, once a week."

***

Notes:

"That show" was the Lord Mayor's annual entertainment.

At its first performances, this play was performed only once a week, on Saturdays.

— NOTES —

— 1.2 —

[*Sings*] '*Thus whilst she sleeps I sorrow for her sake,*' etc.
(1.2.7)
Source of Above:
The Cambridge Edition of the Works of Ben Jonson
7 Volume Set. Volume 2.
Ben Jonson (Author), David Bevington (Editor), Martin Butler (Editor), Ian Donaldson (Editor).
Cambridge University Press, 2012. Print. P. 554.
The song is "Sleep wayward thoughts" by John Dowland and is from his *The First Booke of Songs or Ayres* (1597):

> *Sleep wayward thoughts, and rest you with my love,*
> *Let not my Love be with my love diseas'd.*
> *Touch not proud hands, least you her anger move,*
> *But pine you with my longings displeas'd.*
> *Thus while she sleeps I sorrow for her sake,*
> *So sleeps my Love, and yet my love doth wake.*
> *But on the fury of my restless fear,*
> *The hidden anguish of my flesh desires,*
> *The glories and the beauties that appear,*
> *Between her brows near Cupid's closed fires*
> *Thus while she sleeps I sorrow for her sake,*
> *So sleeps my Love, and yet my love doth wake.*
> *My love doth rage, and yet my Love doth rest,*
> *Fear in my love, and yet my Love secure,*
> *Peace in my Love, and yet my love oppress'd,*
> *Impatient yet of perfect temperature,*
> *Sleep dainty Love, while I sigh for thy sake,*
> *So sleeps my Love, and yet my love doth wake.*

Source: karaoke. Accessed 17 July 2022

https://www.karaoke-lyrics.net/lyrics/dowland-john/sleep-wayward-thoughts-540641

— 3.2 —

But a little higher, but a little higher, but a little higher,
    There, there, there lies Cupid's fire.
(3.2.35-36)
Source of Above:
The Cambridge Edition of the Works of Ben Jonson
7 Volume Set. Volume 2.
Ben Jonson (Author), David Bevington (Editor), Martin Butler (Editor),
Ian Donaldson (Editor).
Cambridge University Press, 2012. Print. P. 583.
The lines are from a bawdy poem by Thomas Campion:

XXII.
Beauty, since you so much desire
To know the place of Cupids fire,
About you somewhere doth it rest,
Yet neuer harbour'd in your brest,
Nor gout-like in your heele or toe ;
What foole would seeke Loues flame so low?
But a little higher, but a little higher,
There, there, ô there lyes Cupids fire.

Thinke not, when Cupid most you scorne,
Men iudge that you of Ice were borne ;
For though you cast loue at your heele,
His fury yet sometime you feele :
And where-abouts if you would know,
I tell you still not in your toe :
But a little higher, but a little higher,
There, there, ô there lyes Cupids fire.

Source of Above: Thomas Campion, *The Third and Fourth Bookes of Ayres:*
The Fourth Booke. Luminarium. Accessed 21 July 2022
http://www.luminarium.org/renlit/beautysince.htm

— 3.2 —

GERTRUDE

> [*Sings*]
> "*His head as white as milk,*
> "*All flaxen was his hair;* 65
> "*But now he is dead,*
> "*And laid in his bed,*
> "*And never will come again.*"
> (3.2-64-68)
> Source of Above:
> *The Cambridge Edition of the Works of Ben Jonson*
> 7 Volume Set. Volume 2.

Ben Jonson (Author), David Bevington (Editor), Martin Butler (Editor), Ian Donaldson (Editor).

> Cambridge University Press, 2012. Print. P. 584.
> In *Hamlet* 4.5, Ophelia sings:

> "*And will he not come again?*
> "*And will he not come again?*
> "*No, no, he is dead:*
> "*Go to thy death-bed:*
> "*He never will come again.*
> "*His beard was as white as snow,*
> "*All flaxen was his poll:*
> "*He is gone, he is gone,*
> "*And we cast away moan:*
> "*God ha' mercy on his soul!*
> "*And of all Christian souls, I pray God. God be wi' ye.*"

Source of Above: Shakespeare, Hamlet. MIT. Accessed 21 July 2022 http://shakespeare.mit.edu/hamlet/full.html

Here are some relevant *Oxford English Dictionary* definitions for "head":

"A person's hair; the whole mass or body of this." (head, n.1, 5a)

"The rounded part forming the end of the penis; the glans." (head, n.1, 18d)

"An accumulation of foam or froth on the top of certain drinks, esp. beer." (head, n.1, 20a)

"The cream which accumulates on the top of milk." (head, n.1, 20b, first citation: 1864)

The *Oxford English Dictionary* also begins a definition of "milk" as "A whitish fluid."

Since the person's hair is flaxen (pale yellowish-gray), and the person's head is "white as milk," the person's head is probably semen.

<h1 style="text-align:center">— 5.1 —</h1>

[*Sings*] '*O hone, hone, o no nera, etc.*'

(5.1.6)

Source of Above:

The Cambridge Edition of the Works of Ben Jonson

7 Volume Set. Volume 2.

Ben Jonson (Author), David Bevington (Editor), Martin Butler (Editor), Ian Donaldson (Editor).

Cambridge University Press, 2012. Print. P. 619.

A song exists that is titled "Franklin" and is sung to the tune "Franklin is fled away":

> *Franklin, my loyal friend,*
> *O hone, O hone!*
> *In whom my joys do end*
> *O hone! O hone!*
> *Franklin, my heart's delight,*
> *Since last he took his flight*
> *Bids now the world goodnight.*
> *O hone, O hone!*

Source: "Franklin." Accessed 17 July 2022

https://universitypublishingonline.org/cambridge/benjonson/static/music/pdf/P.3.6.pdf

The Irish *ochoin* means "oh, alas!"

According to the *Oxford English Dictionary*, the word "franklin" can mean, allusively, "A liberal host."

If that is the case here, it could refer ironically to her father, Touchstone, who no longer takes care of Gertrude.

According to the *Oxford English Dictionary*, the word "franklin" can mean "A freeholder; in 14-15th centuries the designation of a class of landowners, of free but not noble birth, and ranking next below the gentry."

But if "franklin" means "a free landholder," then it could refer ironically to Sir Petronel, who sold Gertrude's land and abandoned her. Of course, he is a knight, but he was not born a knight. Sir Petronel, however, is not free: He is in prison.

The phrase "o no nera" could mean "oh, no ne'ra," aka "oh, no nearer."

Thomas Robinson has a song titled "O Hone" (1609), the music to which these words were set:

O hone, hone, o no nera, O hone, hone, o no nera.

Source: Ross W. Duffin, *Some Other Note: The Lost Songs of English Renaissance Comedy.*

"Nera" is a warrior in Irish Mythology.

> **Nera** *(modern spelling **Neara**) is a warrior of Connacht in the Ulster Cycle of Irish mythology who appears in the 10th cen Middle Irish story the Echtra Nerai.*

Source: "Nera (mythology)." Wikipedia. Accessed 27 July 2022 https://en.wikipedia.org/wiki/Nera_(mythology)

If this is the meaning that Ben Jonson meant, then yes, Sir Petronel is no warrior.

"O no nera" may mean "oh, non-era."

The *Oxford English Dictionary* defines "era" as "A date, or an event, which forms the commencement of a new period in the history of a nation, an institution, individual, art or science, etc.; a memorable or important date." The first citation, however, is 1703.

The *Oxford English Dictionary* defines "non" as "a prohibition." The sole citation is from 1551.

The *Oxford English Dictionary* also defines "non" as "a person who dissents or disapproves." The first citation is 1663.

An *era* can be a beginning of a new period in someone's life and it can be a period in someone's life, and a *non* can be a disapproving person.

The answer that I think is correct is that "O no nera" means "oh, non-era."

Gertrude's life has changed, and she has begun a period in her life in which many people, and especially her father, disapprove of her.

— 5.1 —

Thou wert

afire to be a lady, and now your ladyship and you may both blow at the coal,

(5.1.93-94)

Source of Above:

The Cambridge Edition of the Works of Ben Jonson

7 Volume Set. Volume 2.

Ben Jonson (Author), David Bevington (Editor), Martin Butler (Editor), Ian Donaldson (Editor).

Cambridge University Press, 2012. Print. P. 623.

A Scottish proverb stated, "Let them that are cold blow at the coal."

Another Scottish proverb stated, "It's a cold coal to blow at."

Source: The above Scottish proverbs are from this book:

A Collection of Scotch Proverbs. By Anonymous. Collected by Pappity Stampoy. 1663.

Available at Guttenberg.org:

https://www.gutenberg.org/files/7018/7018-h/7018-h.htm

Appendix A: About the Author

It was a dark and stormy night. Suddenly a cry rang out, and on a hot summer night in 1954, Josephine, wife of Carl Bruce, gave birth to a boy — me. Unfortunately, this young married couple allowed Reuben Saturday, Josephine's brother, to name their first-born. Reuben, aka "The Joker," decided that Bruce was a nice name, so he decided to name me Bruce Bruce. I have gone by my middle name — David — ever since.

Being named Bruce David Bruce hasn't been all bad. Bank tellers remember me very quickly, so I don't often have to show an ID. It can be fun in charades, also. When I was a counselor as a teenager at Camp Echoing Hills in Warsaw, Ohio, a fellow counselor gave the signs for "sounds like" and "two words," then she pointed to a bruise on her leg twice. Bruise Bruise? Oh yeah, Bruce Bruce is the answer!

Uncle Reuben, by the way, gave me a haircut when I was in kindergarten. He cut my hair short and shaved a small bald spot on the back of my head. My mother wouldn't let me go to school until the bald spot grew out again.

Of all my brothers and sisters (six in all), I am the only transplant to Athens, Ohio. I was born in Newark, Ohio, and have lived all around Southeastern Ohio. However, I moved to Athens to go to Ohio University and have never left.

At Ohio U, I never could make up my mind whether to major in English or Philosophy, so I got a bachelor's degree with a double major in both areas, then I added a Master of Arts degree in English and a Master of Arts degree in Philosophy. Yes, I have my MAMA degree.

Currently, and for a long time to come (I eat fruits and veggies), I am spending my retirement writing books such as *Nadia Comaneci: Perfect 10*, *The Funniest People in Comedy*, *Homer's* Iliad: *A Retelling in Prose*, and *William Shakespeare's* Hamlet: *A Retelling in Prose*.

If all goes well, I will publish one or two books a year for the rest of my life. (On the other hand, a good way to make God laugh is to tell Her your plans.)

By the way, my sister Brenda Kennedy writes romances such as *A New Beginning* and *Shattered Dreams*.

Appendix B: Some Books by David Bruce

Retellings of a Classic Work of Literature

Arden of Faversham*: A Retelling*

Ben Jonson's The Alchemist: *A Retelling*

Ben Jonson's The Arraignment, or Poetaster: *A Retelling*

Ben Jonson's Bartholomew Fair: *A Retelling*

Ben Jonson's The Case is Altered: *A Retelling*

Ben Jonson's Catiline's Conspiracy: *A Retelling*

Ben Jonson's The Devil is an Ass: *A Retelling*

Ben Jonson's Epicene: *A Retelling*

Ben Jonson's Every Man in His Humor: *A Retelling*

Ben Jonson's Every Man Out of His Humor: *A Retelling*

Ben Jonson's The Fountain of Self-Love, or Cynthia's Revels: *A Retelling*

Ben Jonson's The Magnetic Lady, or Humors Reconciled: *A Retelling*

Ben Jonson's The New Inn, or The Light Heart: *A Retelling*

Ben Jonson's Sejanus' Fall: *A Retelling*

Ben Jonson's The Staple of News: *A Retelling*

Ben Jonson's A Tale of a Tub: *A Retelling*

Ben Jonson's Volpone, or the Fox: *A Retelling*

Christopher Marlowe's Complete Plays: Retellings

Christopher Marlowe's Dido, Queen of Carthage: *A Retelling*

Christopher Marlowe's Doctor Faustus: *Retellings of the 1604 A-Text and of the 1616 B-Text*

Christopher Marlowe's Edward II: *A Retelling*

Christopher Marlowe's The Massacre at Paris: *A Retelling*

Christopher Marlowe's The Rich Jew of Malta: *A Retelling*

Christopher Marlowe's Tamburlaine, Parts 1 and 2: *Retellings*

Dante's Divine Comedy: *A Retelling in Prose*

Dante's Inferno: *A Retelling in Prose*

Dante's Purgatory: *A Retelling in Prose*

Dante's Paradise: *A Retelling in Prose*

The Famous Victories of Henry V: *A Retelling*

From the Iliad *to the* Odyssey: *A Retelling in Prose of Quintus of Smyrna's* Posthomerica

George Chapman, Ben Jonson, and John Marston's Eastward Ho! *A Retelling*

George Peele's The Arraignment of Paris: *A Retelling*

George Peele's The Battle of Alcazar: *A Retelling*

George's Peele's David and Bathsheba, and the Tragedy of Absalom: *A Retelling*

George Peele's Edward I: *A Retelling*

George Peele's The Old Wives' Tale: *A Retelling*

George-a-Greene: *A Retelling*

William Shakespeare's 1 Henry IV, aka Henry IV, Part 1: *A Retelling in Prose*
William Shakespeare's 2 Henry IV, aka Henry IV, Part 2: *A Retelling in Prose*
William Shakespeare's 1 Henry VI, aka Henry VI, Part 1: *A Retelling in Prose*
William Shakespeare's 2 Henry VI, aka Henry VI, Part 2: *A Retelling in Prose*
William Shakespeare's 3 Henry VI, aka Henry VI, Part 3: *A Retelling in Prose*
William Shakespeare's All's Well that Ends Well: *A Retelling in Prose*
William Shakespeare's Antony and Cleopatra: *A Retelling in Prose*
William Shakespeare's As You Like It: *A Retelling in Prose*
William Shakespeare's The Comedy of Errors: *A Retelling in Prose*
William Shakespeare's Coriolanus: *A Retelling in Prose*
William Shakespeare's Cymbeline: *A Retelling in Prose*
William Shakespeare's Hamlet: *A Retelling in Prose*
William Shakespeare's Henry V: *A Retelling in Prose*
William Shakespeare's Henry VIII: *A Retelling in Prose*
William Shakespeare's Julius Caesar: *A Retelling in Prose*
William Shakespeare's King John: *A Retelling in Prose*
William Shakespeare's King Lear: *A Retelling in Prose*
William Shakespeare's Love's Labor's Lost: *A Retelling in Prose*
William Shakespeare's Macbeth: *A Retelling in Prose*
William Shakespeare's Measure for Measure: *A Retelling in Prose*
William Shakespeare's The Merchant of Venice: *A Retelling in Prose*
William Shakespeare's The Merry Wives of Windsor: *A Retelling in Prose*
William Shakespeare's A Midsummer Night's Dream: *A Retelling in Prose*
William Shakespeare's Much Ado About Nothing: *A Retelling in Prose*
William Shakespeare's Othello: *A Retelling in Prose*
William Shakespeare's Pericles, Prince of Tyre: *A Retelling in Prose*
William Shakespeare's Richard II: *A Retelling in Prose*
William Shakespeare's Richard III: *A Retelling in Prose*
William Shakespeare's Romeo and Juliet: *A Retelling in Prose*
William Shakespeare's The Taming of the Shrew: *A Retelling in Prose*
William Shakespeare's The Tempest: *A Retelling in Prose*
William Shakespeare's Timon of Athens: *A Retelling in Prose*
William Shakespeare's Titus Andronicus: *A Retelling in Prose*
William Shakespeare's Troilus and Cressida: *A Retelling in Prose*
William Shakespeare's Twelfth Night: *A Retelling in Prose*
William Shakespeare's The Two Gentlemen of Verona: *A Retelling in Prose*
William Shakespeare's The Two Noble Kinsmen: *A Retelling in Prose*
William Shakespeare's The Winter's Tale: *A Retelling in Prose*